The Samurai

Book One of the Samurai Trilogy

By Luke Dimech

Part 1

Chapter One – My Father, the Peaceful Warrior (Eleven years ago)

I gaze out of the window at my father, Ezekiel. The grey tones of his now drenched robes match the sky. Clouds hang menacingly over the fields of our farm, making it feel like it's later than midday. My father seems un-phased by the weather. He stands as still as the mountains on the horizon. In the heaviness of the rain, all I see is his blurred silhouette, making it impossible to make out his features. I am sure, however, that his eyes are shut, meditating on the situation and the battle that is about to unfold. He has always talked to me about the importance of all the senses. Sight is not the only sense that can aid you in combat, and a good warrior is accustomed to playing tricks on the eyes of an opponent to gain the upper hand, tricks that would fail should you harness all of your senses. The sword, *Senso*, glints, even in today's darkness. The sword has been with our family for an age. My father has always told me that a warrior's sword should be an extension of himself.

'It is taught that a sword is the most important aspect of the warrior, more important than even his family, lands or food.' He would then laugh at me when my expression turned to shock. 'Don't worry my son, you are more important to me than my sword, but only just.' He would wink at me and smile.

A roar forces its way through the downpour. I watch three men approach my father in haste, yet he is steadfast. He is listening and waiting for his moment. A split-second feels like an entire turn of the sun. The first of the three, who wields a dull blade with blue garb and a leather breastplate protecting his upper body, approaches with wide, crazed eyes. Father lifts his sword in a fluid motion, the blade flashes as if the sun had reflected off the perfect weapon; how does that happen when all around us is grey? With that single moment, the first attacker drops to his knees, blood pouring from his neck. He falls face-first into the muddy ground. Father switches to a defensive stance and observes the two remaining enemies. The shock on their faces apparent. I can tell they have lost the fight already. Honour would drive them to continue.

The distinct blue clothing marks these warriors as members of the Tashendi tribe. The Tashendi are supposed to birth fighters, giving them their first sword on their sixth birthday. My father outmatches them easily. His speed and skill surpass even the best of them easily. They try a new tactic as the first and older member of the posse shifts sideways to flank. They must figure that my father cannot defend from both sides how silly they are. Usually, this is against the rules of combat. One-on-one is the accepted and trusted way of duelling. The minds of men who are fearing for their life changes those rules. I wonder, though, if they did, by some miracle, defeat my father, would the friends fight each other next, or perhaps the one who strikes truest will keep the blade? The glory and sword cannot be shared by two.

They both charge him simultaneously, and in two flashes of *Senso,* he has parried one attack and sliced the head off the second, who now lies on the ground, lifeless. My father then spins off the advance of the third and final warrior. The enemies blade misses by mere inches, and he lurches forward in attack. *Senso* moves too swiftly, almost supernaturally in the hands of my father, as the tip of the sword connects with the top of his enemy's spine, severing the nerves attached to the brain. He falls, unable to move, shaking as the life leaks from his body. Father bows to each and drives the blade through the final warrior's head, giving him a swift and honourable death.

Father whips the blade of *Senso* to remove any excess blood and then sheaths the weapon in the same beautiful motion as if he had just painted a masterpiece. He turns to me; a soft smile appears on his face. However, I see the pain in his eyes for having to take another life. It is his blessing and his curse to be the most renowned warrior these lands have ever seen.

Father walks back to the house. I turn away from the window and see my mother, Telaá, preparing some tea for him. Jasmine and Chamomile, a calming tea. I see nothing of the aggression I witnessed in my father as he glides in and takes his seat at the table. I would never imagine that the scene only moments ago was that of chaos and bloodshed. They look at each other, saying nothing. She touches his face, and for a moment, they forget that I am here. I don't mind this. I can only hope that I find someone equal to my mother when I am older. She was once a great warrior too. That is how they met - duelling each other. They once told me the story of how they fought for hours. Neither one of them could strike true. They fell in love fighting. They realised that it was that same love that stopped them from harming each other. When I was born, father gave her a choice to be the warrior or the mother, or he the father, not the warrior. She wanted to look after me, and so she gave up her sword. They still spar sometimes; mother likes to stay sharp.

'How did it go, my love?' my mother asks.

'The usual; I try to warn them, plead with them not to fight. They don't listen.'

'They never do.'

My father looks at me. 'Jacob, I am sorry.'

'Sorry? For what father?'

'That this sword will be your burden one day if I am not defeated before you earn the right to wield *Senso*.'

I look at him and smile, 'Defeated; father, you are funny. You will not be defeated ever. You are the strongest man in the world.'

Chapter Two – Training the Beginning (Ten years ago)

I sit in the kitchen, waiting in the darkness. All the lamps have been snuffed out, and I can feel the excitement rising as my heart pounds frantically in my chest. I sit, attempting to be patient, and I see the first flickers of light coming from the other room. I clasp my hands together, feeling the blood draining from my fingertips as they start to turn cold. I know this is the beginning; this is what my father and I have been waiting for my entire life. 'Father, Mother! Come on, where are you?' I shout. I hear a voice break the silence and darkness from the other room.

'Not long now,' laughs Ezekiel.

I wait for what seems another year. It is my tenth birthday, which means just one thing to me. Tomorrow, I can start training with my father. I have been watching him my entire childhood, and I want to do what he does. Suddenly the light from the other room starts flickering towards me. The eagerness threatens to make me lose control, my father would be disappointed if it did, so I stand firm. My parents walk into the room, cake in hand, and I cannot tell if it is the reflections of candle fire or if excitement is blazing in their eyes, much like my own.

The cake is a wonderfully finished Samurai. He wears armour crafted from icing and is crouched beside a Sakura tree, shaded pink with the scent of strawberries. The blade of his sword made from sugar. It is a work of art that takes my breath away and looks too good to eat.

'This is lovely,' I say while gently poking the sword.

'Happy birthday, son,' they say in unison.

My father seizes a knife from the table and shears the cake into strips — plating three and giving me the largest piece. I stare at it and await permission to tuck into this sweet feast.

'What are you waiting for?' My mother asks.

'Permission!'

Father laughs heartily. 'It is your tenth birthday; you no longer need permission to eat cake. I smile and commence devouring the samurai, sword and all. The sweetness floods my taste buds.

Strawberry and vanilla flavour ignites my senses as I chew. My mother is magic; I am sure of it.

We eat until most of the cake is gone, I feel sick, but I dare not tell my parents as they would taunt me for overeating. I go to bed excited for tomorrow's beginning; I can start my training with the sword as my father promised, maybe, if I do well, I will get a sword of my own.

I wake in the morning and leap out of bed. Wash as quickly as I can and race through the house to the garden.

'Jacob!' I hear my mother call me. I race back inside, panting with motivation. 'A warrior does not train on an empty stomach.'

My mother is, of course, right. I sit impatiently and await my breakfast. She makes me two eggs, instead of my usual one, combining it with a large portion of sticky rice, still warm from the hob. I stab a knife into the runny eggs, they are delicious, and I scoff it all. I am an adult now and must eat like one to be healthy for training.

'I finished it, Mother.'

'Ok, off you go then. Good luck out there.'
She winks at me, and I bow back then hurry outside
to find my master, my father.

I see him already training and make my way
to the great tree which overhangs the sheep pens. He
strikes an imaginary opponent over and over,
occasionally shifting his weight or changing his
angle. One thousand of each sword stroke a day;
that's what he has told me in the past. The sweat
starts to drip off his face, yet I see nothing but
tranquillity in his eyes. He pauses and looks at me,
smiling.

The first question that pops into my head is a
strange one. 'Why do you tell me that you love me
more than your sword? Isn't that wrong?'

'Because a warrior with nothing to fight for
finds it easy to die.' His response confuses me at first.
After a short moment, I realise what that means and
am overwhelmed by the responsibility of keeping him
alive. He turns back around and settles into a new
stance. *Senso* is a part of him, and he it, you can tell
by his movements. They flow as one. The kata he
uses looks like a deadly dance. He pierces the air,

spinning, slicing, and jumping all in harmony. I find a stick under the tree and attempt to replicate my father's movements. The fence post of the pens becomes my enemy, and I charge it swinging wildly. I hack and swing, yet the post does not falter. My arms start to ache from the vibrations of wood on wood, and still, the fence post moves but barely an inch. I cease the attack, panting and catching my breath. Fighting is hard work! I turn to see my father looking at me. He drops to a knee and places his hand on my shoulder, 'Jacob, a battle is not won with rage.' He stands back up and focuses on *Senso*. 'It's about control combined with fluidity.'

He shifts forward into a dance with his blade. Like a great dancer, leading his partner in a practised precision, he spins and turns as if dodging an opponent with great ease. Swiftly and suddenly, his feet grow firm, and he takes a single swipe at the fence post. My eyes barely keep up. How does he move so quickly? I stare in awe as the top section of the post slides off the bottom. It is a perfect cut. It is as if the wood has been sanded and finished by a master carpenter.

'That was amazing; it is no wonder you are feared.'

Ezekiel's face drops slightly. 'Son, I did not become a warrior to be feared,' He looks me in the eye and pats my head. 'To be feared is to be a tyrant. I am capable because I understand man's nature and his desire to fight. I train hard to protect those in need.'

'We have soldiers for that father. No one fights like that anymore, do they?'

'History shows us that all men are flawed. Rules are written, much like the ones made to protect us all, and yes, the majority do follow them. However, if cornered, any man can become a beast.' He places his hands on my shoulders, 'I train and practice for hours each day so that if such a beast should attack the innocent or seek to cause harm to my people or family, I can defend them. I fight, so they don't have to.' His eyes soften, his smile reappearing.

'I... I understand, father.' He grins and ruffles my hair.

'Are you sure you just turned ten? You are already wiser than some of the sages I have met.' There is a slight pause like he is giving himself a moment to memorise this conversation. 'Now Jacob, tell me, oh wise one, what lesson did you learn today?'

I look away to contemplate my answer. 'Erm, I think angry people do not make good warriors.'

'A strong answer and a true statement, but not the one I was searching for.'

'_____' My father waits for me to make a second attempt. I search my brain for the right thing to say. I know he won't judge me if I get it wrong. He is not that kind of man. I do, however, want to make him proud.

He interrupts the silence, and I kick myself for not speaking sooner. 'The lesson you learnt today is that losing self-control is costly. For instance, your loss of control caused the fence post to get sliced in two. It now needs replacing, or else our livestock will wander free.'

'But you sliced it, not I!'

'That is correct, but why did I slice it?'

'To show me how to be in control...' I say slowly.

'Exactly. Therefore, your actions caused an equal reaction that turned out to be unfavourable not only to you but the world around you also.'

I understand him completely and rush off to collect another fence post and shovel. The post is so heavy that I stumble. My father is soon with me, helping me to carry them over. We work quickly together and replace the fence. I learnt the lesson today.

After a few days of constant sword drills, my body is numb. My aches make it challenging to get myself out of bed, and my hunger is never sated. This morning I feel more drawn to the paintings in my room. Each of my four walls has an image of an element attached to it, pictures that my mother created. She is as adept with a brush as she is a blade. She prefers the gentler art these days. Directly in front of my bed is an image of the rising sun. It is the first thing I see when I wake. It always makes me feel warm, even when the snow covers the lands. It is my favourite of all her paintings. The hues of yellow, orange and red, cresting over a green horizon. It warms the silhouetted figures walking the distant path below the ball of fire. To the left is an image of leaves blowing in the wind. The green and brown leaves of an autumn fall, swirling and playing with the gusts. My father would tell me that the wind can be your greatest enemy, yet with a slight change in direction, your greatest ally. Stand against the wind on your journey, and it will make it feel ten times the distance. Harness the wind on your journey, and you will cut the trip in half. Run with the wind, and you will know the meaning of haste. To my right, an image of an older man standing in the rain. I asked my father repeatedly about this image; it has always confused me.

'Why does he stand in the rain and not seek shelter?'

'Rain is water, and water is life. Without it, we and the earth we live on would perish. Everything you see relies on it. Why should we cower and hide away from something that brings so much life for the sake of dry clothes? This is folly son, rain whispers to us of greatness. She shows us that all life focuses on it. We can only survive three days without water, yet three weeks without food.'

I now understand that older man. He is not caught in a storm; he is embracing it. Feeling every drop strike his face and giving life — each a small gift to the earth. Finally, on the wall behind me is a great storm, tendrils of rain combined with the yellow flashes of lightning.

I have been told stories of the past, how man used to harness electricity's energy, powering large cities, giving light in the dark and powering great vehicles. Lightning represents change and often comes at the altering of a season. As winter spars with summer, the heat versus the cold, the elements produce fireworks. My mother often describes it as a dance. The seasons meet twice a year, enjoying each other's company for a fleeting moment, parading with respect for each other. They know one cannot live without the other and embrace it with love. She also tells me that a really long time ago, people used to worship gods that they say caused such scenes. A pagan god called Thor, a great warrior who created the lightening by hitting his magical hammer against a giant anvil. A story I love.

I feel lucky to wake to such images and stories. I have always been fascinated by such things. I have sat in the rain, the beaming sun, the winds that have blown past my house, and watched the storms upon the mountains. Each one makes me feel alive. Today the sun floods through my window. I can feel its warmth piercing through the gaps in my window already.

I can already smell breakfast, and I do not doubt that my father and mother have been up preparing for the day. I stretch, and it momentarily eases the aches in my body, yet as soon as I stop, the pain returns. It is a good pain. I rush to the kitchen and take a seat at the table.

'Have you washed, Jacob?' my mother asks.

I get up and race to the bathroom; the food smells so good my stomach grumbles at the delay. As I walk past my parent's room, I notice my father meditating. I stop and peer through the crack in the door. He is holding *Senso* in his lap. I rarely see him without his blade. He seems to spend more time with it than with Mother. He sits cross-legged facing the window. He is humming words; I cannot quite make out what they are. Suddenly yet slowly, he lifts *Senso*, his arms outstretched at shoulder height. It almost seems like he is offering it to an invisible master. The sun peers through the shuttered window, enveloping my father. The warmth of the room rises. I am not sure if it is my imagination. I watch my father; the words are like a song, he chants the lyrics, and I notice the repetition – 'Taiyō' he is chanting to the sun! He is chanting to the sun. I see something strange; my father seems to be floating a few inches off the floor. This cannot be. Surely it is a trick of the light? Suddenly a bright light flashing off my father's blade, blinding me. I look away, the white flash leaving a glow in my eyesight as if I had looked at the sun for too long. I blink once to try and remove the glow, and within that blink, my father is upon me, sword pointed at my neck.

'Spying on me, son,' he chuckles.

'No, father. It was just amazing, it is like the sun was talking to you and you to it.'

'Tell me, what do you think you saw?'

'You, asking the sun to make you fly? You were already floating. I saw it!'

'As I always say, my son, the weather is your friend if you understand how to use it. It may look like I was floating, but that's because the sunlight tricked you: and I knew you were watching me, so with a flash of light off my blade, I was upon you in a flash, like I would be an enemy should they attempt to fight me in the sunlight.'

I feel disappointment at his response. I had hoped it was true. I wish my father could fly.

After a breakfast of eggs and rice balls, I place the dishes into the sink gently and rush off to meet my father outside. Leaning on the door is the stick I had been using as a sword the previous mornings. I see my father by the tree waiting for my arrival, but first, I wanted to try something. I sneak back into my room, stick in hand. I find a good spot where the sun is warming the floor and sit cross-legged as my father had done. I close my eyes and try to remember the rhythm of the chant. 'Taiyō, Taiyō, Taiyō,' I mutter, trying to give it the same guttural hum my father had managed. Am I doing this right? I feel nothing but the warmth of the sun on my face, the stick placed in my lap. Of course! I must offer it. I lift my hand, shoulder high, offering my make-do-sword in front of me. The sun does not respond. It caresses the skin on my face like it always does when you sit directly in it. I continue to hum the words. My mind drifts, and I start to think about training, but I must focus. I bring myself back, but nothing happens. My impatience grows. 'I am offering the sun a stick, not a sword. That won't make me fly, offering such a stupid thing.' Giving up, I race outside. I notice that my aches and pains have gone, energy has filled my body, and I feel ready to train.

My father is outside, sitting cross-legged, with *Senso* perched on his shoulder. He looks at me disapproving as I exit the house. 'Why have you not started training father?'

'I was awaiting the arrival of my student. A teacher cannot teach someone who is not there,' he laughs to himself.

'Sorry father, I was just trying to fly as you did, but all I had to offer the sun was this little stick.'

'Well, we must do something about that. We can't have you offering a stick to the sun God.' He stands and grabs something from behind the tree. A training sword, sheathed and carved from oak. It is beautiful. The elemental signs are inscribed on the hilt, and it looks brand new.

'Is this for me?'

'Yes, I have been working on it for a while now, and the lacquer had to dry solid before you could use it. I have made it from one of the branches of this great tree.' He hands me the wooden sword. It is so much heavier than my stick. I try a few practice swings, and I instantly fall in love. He falls in line next to me, and we begin to practice our swings and strikes.

The day is a long one. The weight of the new sword takes its toll on my muscles. My shoulders burn from all the repetition, and both my father and I sweat a lot. Thankfully, not a single fence post was destroyed today. The sun starts to descend. Its amber glow warms the land, making the ground look like its burning. Greens turn yellow, and the grass looks like an ocean of barley fields, swaying with each light breeze. The mountain on the horizon casts a shadow towards us. The sun brightens its entire face. My father signals for the end of today's training. 'You have done very well to keep training with such a heavy new blade. Tomorrow, you can have the day off to play with your friends and relax.'

'Why would I want to do that?'

'Because it's fun,' Ezekiel exclaimed.

'So is training, plus I won't improve if I waste time playing games, will I?'

My father looks at me, smiling softly. 'You shall be a great master one day my son. Of this, I have no doubt.'

I bow to my father and raise my sword requesting a duel.

'Have we not trained enough?' He asks.

'Just a quick fight father, I want to try my moves.'

He bows back at me, lifting *Senso* in a defensive stance. He closes his eyes as he does at the beginning of every duel.

Chapter Three – Training Strength Incarnate (Four years ago)

Six years of solid training, no breaks, no holding back, just training. I have loved it. My sword flows effortlessly as an extension of my being. I can now keep up with my father's swings and strikes, and we spend most of our time sparring. Today is different. Today is my sixteenth birthday. It is time to extend my training to more than swordplay. It is time to work on my senses. My Father, Master Ezekiel as I now call him, has been preparing, and in this time, have mastered the blade dance, and the katas have become second nature. He explains to me that it took him at least ten years to learn them, and I feel a sense of pride ooze through me. All I want is to make him proud, and I think I have achieved that so far. If I can master my senses in the same way, I will be a master; then I can start duelling for real.

'Lesson one, Jacob,' he says to me. 'Sit by the tree, close your eyes, and tell me what you feel.'

I close my eyes and take a deep breath. The inhalation brings with it all the smells and sounds in the fields that surround me. The grass oozing the damp smells of the morning, playing in the breeze, swinging left and right, bending and swaying but never breaking. The sheep are chewing and conversing with each other, trotting around the fields. I wonder how much they notice of the world outside their own? The lingering smells of breakfast, the food we just ate and my beautiful mother singing to herself, I wonder if she watches us? The breeze shifts. I feel it push towards me. Something is changing. I open my eyes and see my father standing in front of me, *Senso* pointing at my throat, ready for the kill.

'Did you feel that?' he asks.

'I felt a shift on the wind father.'

'Yes, that is good. I caused that shift. As I approached you in haste, the breeze shifted and warned you of my advance.'

'I understand.'

'You must react considerably faster to those shifts,' he explains to me. 'Now you must run. Run towards the next village, and once you have gone as far as you can, you must run back. At the same time, I want you to remember your environment. The sounds, the smells, the creatures you pass. Once you are back, you must duel me.'

'What! That sounds crazy; the next village is over four hours of jogging.'

'Yes, that is correct. Once you can run there, back and still duel me, you will be a master.'

It seems like an impossible task, yet I know my father. He would not give me such an exercise if it were not achievable. He makes me believe it. His soft eyes tell me that it is an attainable task and that he would never ask the impossible of me. He throws me some food, wrapped in cloth and a small backpack in which to carry it.

'You will need this.'

I take the bag, place the food inside along with some water skins and start to run. I take a moment to look back at my father. He watches me still, a proud look on his face. It makes me want to run faster. I must be the Master he tells me I can become. He watches me with such observant eyes, always making me believe I can achieve anything. To this day, he has not been wrong. The only one who seems to have doubts is me. I don't know how he does it.

I run for what feels like an entire season, making my way past the isolated farmsteads of our distant neighbours. They wave to me as I pass, smiling away like they know what my father is making me go through. My legs start to burn; this is very different from the standard training. If I can only last ten minutes of combat and become winded, I will be useless. I must be good at everything. Strength alone is futile without stamina and sheer will. My legs urge me forward, but my brain is starting to tell me I am stupid for continuing. I decide I must turn back at six miles; else I won't even make it home in a crawl and be in no state to spar with father.

As I make my way back, the rain starts to fall. Great, now I must get soaked too. I try to remember the older man in my mother's painting, accepting the rain and all the life that comes with it. The hard ground becomes soft, and it is becoming far more challenging to stay upright. My feet slip, and I must look foolish, flailing my limbs to stay up. I approach the edge of a hill, the final stretch home. As soon as I take a step forward, my heel denies me the solid footing I was expecting. My feet slide away from under me, and I roll, rather ungracefully down the hill, body splashing into the mud, leaving a spray of dirty water coating my face. Thankfully, no sharp rocks were on this slimy route back to the house. I quickly stand up at the bottom, glancing around to check no one has seen my mishap. It would seem I got away with it, that was until I made it home. My father is laughing hysterically, grabbing his belly as if he has an upset stomach. 'What happened?' he chuckles, 'did you fight with a mud monster on the way?'

'I... I slipped,' I say, looking down at my mud-soaked attire.

'Don't worry; you will get used to the route and the perilous monsters you will meet along the way.'

Before I have the chance to feel sorry for myself, my father draws his sword and attacks. My legs almost give way as I attempt a last-second retreat. He keeps coming, relentlessly swinging his blade. I parry as well as I can, but I'm left on the back foot. I feel my balance starting to give way, and he smashes his blade into my training sword, the final push that makes me once again bathe in mud. His attacks stop. He sheaths his sword and holds out his hand. 'I think you have had enough today, son,' He lifts me off the floor and bows, walking back into the house with nothing else to say. I can only imagine how much effort it will take to run the return trip and successfully spar with him. I trudge back into the house, careful not to get mud everywhere. The last thing I want right now is a spar with my mother too.

The running gets more comfortable every day. A few weeks in, and I can already run double that of the first day. I am getting used to the route and environment. Now I see the fields; I know which ones are wheat and which are corn, which are grazing spots and for which animals. I know that when I get within a mile of the pig farm, I can smell it, dependant on the wind direction. I know when the neighbours are cooking and what. I know that when the wind blows east, the run to town is painless, but the run back more difficult, and I also know which path to take should it rain, and of course, which way to avoid. My balance and stamina improve significantly, and I feel stronger;

it feels like a long time ago that I struggled with the route.

The sunny days are the easiest; it is almost like it powers me. Where all the trampled grass has turned to mud, a path has started forming. It extends to the plains of our lands and pushes all the way to the town. I have grown used to the scenery now, but not sick of it. I run at a pace that still gives me time to observe it all, soaking in every tree, every change in the wind and every smell, hearing the footsteps that are not my own; the rabbits, the deer and other animals that hide in the shadows. My father says running is not just training for your heart and stamina, but training for all your senses. He talks about how a warrior must not rely on vision alone in combat but must rely on everything. Changes to familiar smells can alert the brain of danger. Similarly, a beautiful, exotic perfume crafted from the richest blossoms can cause the brain to ignite, as does the stench of a warrior who has travelled for days for a chance to fight. A journey that is boring to a regular man turns into sensory overload.

I know and feel like I am getting close to the village. I can potentially make it all the way and return home, but will I have enough energy for combat? Being in a battle cannot be a sprint. It must be calm and collected. If you use all your power on the first man, then the second one will kill you. One must learn to judge the effort you put into the initial stages of combat and predict your opponents' fierceness, thus giving yourself a stronger chance of survival and energy to defeat them all. If an entire group decides that they want your sword and title, then you could end up fighting them all.

I grow used to the run and fighting my father, yet on this occasion, I am surprised to find my mother awaiting me. I run over, thinking that something must have happened to my father.

'Mother, is everything ok?'

She smiles at me, her soft, warm eyes filling me with love. She unsheathes her sword and races towards me. Her smile changes, her eyes switch to that of a hawk, and I am forced to defend myself against a very different opponent. I thought my father was fast, but she is another level of nimble. She glides in every direction; her feet don't seem to touch the floor. She flows like a surging river but with the grace of a gazelle. She makes it difficult for me to block her strikes. A flurry of attacks fly past me. She thrusts like a viper, her blade glinting off the hot sun in a constant flash of strikes. I can tell that she doesn't hold the same strength as my father, but her speed is deadly. I manage to seize my footing and roll to the side, hoping to catch her off guard. By the time I am standing, she is already in a defensive position. How do you defeat such speed!

I charge her, she turns away and starts to run, she must fear my power, I persist as she runs to the house. She reaches the fence and jumps. I thought she was leaping over it in an attempt to slow me down, but I am wrong. Her feet hit the fence, and she flips right over my head, slashing out with her sword, catching the front of my shirt. I stop and look down, seeing a big slice out of my clothing.

'Don't worry, I will sew that up for you,' she says to me, smiling.

I focus myself and swing heavily, relying on my strength to overcome her speed. She ducks my blows easily and slices my bootstraps as I step out of my shoe. She chuckles to herself, and I am forced to concede. 'You could have defeated me at any time, Mother.'

'Well, actually, you put on a masterful fight, plus I was cheating.'

'Cheating? How?'

'You will find out one day Jacob, just know that you are already an impressive warrior.' She bows to me and gestures for my sliced shirt. 'Come on then, let me sew that up.'

Chapter Four – The Awakening (Two Years Ago)

I make my way back from another run, my legs burning, heart and senses racing, holding focus on the surroundings is still a challenge when nearing the end of these long-distance jaunts. I find it hard to think about anything but my legs, as the lactic acid takes grasp and causes them to slow. I defiantly press forward, rebelling against my brain and refusing to allow my pace to lag. It would be easy to give up and walk the rest of the way home, but I will gain nothing from that.

The cold rain starts to fall, the drops striking my face, giving me some respite from the heat of the day, cooling my body and making my running somewhat more comfortable. The rain gains fury, water coating the sky, creating a dark grey fortress that surrounds me. The water pours into my eyes, attempting to obscure and blind me. I cannot stop, and I cannot wipe the rain from them. In combat, the moment you leave a defensive position is the moment your opponent can strike. How can my father fight so freely in these conditions? His lessons are always flowing back into my thoughts when a moment of weakness looms over me.

'The stance must hold, no matter what is going on around you, do not let your peripheral vision fool you nor let the elements trick you. Use them instead as your ally; if you learn to harness that discipline, then the weather and environment will always be on your side.'

The route becomes slippery. I am forced to slow from run to a jog. I see lightning in the distance, followed by the low rumbling of thunder seconds after. There is a strange feeling in the air. Someone is watching me. I attempt to ignore it, but the unusual sense becomes too overwhelming to forget. It feels like a thousand eyes examining my every move. I stop to glance around, seeing nothing but fields around me, the grass disinterested by my presence. It merely sways to and fro as it always has. I notice that there are no animals grazing or sheltering under the trees, unusual for this part of the world, especially these fields. Something is not right, yet I do not feel uncomfortable. It is as if someone is watching after me, not stalking me. The only noticeable thing that is approaching is the terrible weather.

Rain is falling hard, and a cloud of grey and black begins to obscure the once blue heavens. Lightning strikes like an angry opponent pounding the ground with fury and electricity. I try to forget the odd feeling and continue to run, but this time making haste. Without being able to sense the cause of this situation, I break into a sprint, the dark clouds growing closer, and the moments between lighting and thunder become just a few seconds apart. The mud and uneven ground tries its best to knock me off balance, threatening a rematch with the mud monster I tangled with previously; I laugh to myself. 'A foe such as this cannot defeat me; I am a balance master, I shall not be slowed!' I shout at the shadow in the sky.

It grows dark, but not because the day is coming to an end but because the thick, rain-filled clouds now shield the sunlight completely. I can barely see the ground in front of me, and the path becomes treacherous, puddles growing into pools of unknown depth. I am forced to go around them just in case the ground within them is unstable. It has become far too dangerous now, so I slow from a jog to a walk, admitting defeat. I remember the old man in the painting on my bedroom wall. He doesn't fight with the rain; he befriends it, allowing its touch to coat him. I slow to a halt embracing the moment, sitting down as the old man teaches. I take this moment to meditate and not fight, accepting the world as it currently is and allowing the elements to take charge. I close my eyes and let my skin, ears and nose take over, flooding them with the relentless patter of rain until it ceases to be my enemy and allowing its rhythm to take hold of my soul. It is so loud that it sounds like the ocean breaking over a shore laden with seashells. The drops savagely hit my body as the wind picks up, trying to blow me over in heavy gusts. I take a crossed-legged posture, hands made into fists at the front of my lap, knuckles touching. It is a robust and low stance to keep me firm in the adverse surroundings.

All I can hear is the wind, rain and thunder. The storm is doing all it can to dampen my mood. Little does it know that these are the moments when I feel my most alive. The feeling of being watched remains, making the hair on the back of my neck prickle up. My defiance to give in seems to make the elements angrier, yet I smile. In a disciplined life, a moment of rebellion is always that much sweeter. It's me versus the weather, something I always enjoy. I remember my mother finding me sitting outside the house in a storm, soaking wet, just staring and observing what was happening, wanting for a moment or two to become the storm itself, to gain some sort of insight as to why we fear it so much. Something so furious yet a blessing to mother nature, one that can destroy but also bring life. I imagine myself as a blade of grass from the field, moving with the wind and soaking up the rain. Without the rain and electricity, lands would die, and crops would fail. Yes, the storm doesn't just bring life; it is life.

My senses completely take over, and my brain stops analysing. I sit and become the storm. I no longer feel cold nor wet; I sway with each gust, allowing them to control me as my body drifts with each grasp and flurry. It goes quiet, eerily and suddenly, the wind has dissipated, and the rain departs, causing me to return to my senses.

'The eye, I am in the eye of the storm,' I realise. I glance around, still sat in my meditative posture as a wall of water surrounds me, so much rain that I can no longer tell if it is coming down or going up. Yet, it has stopped falling on me. It surrounds me like a group of onlookers, waiting for me to act. It is as if I am inside a roofless house made of waterfalls pouring from the heavens. I look up and see the black clouds swirling around a tight circle. Lightning cracks and thunders above my head. It feels strange, like something supernatural.

Perhaps I have passed out and am dreaming? Silence shrouds me despite the falling water, a silence reserved for ancient and dilapidated graveyards that have been forgotten over time; the lightening no longer producing the boom of thunder. I unclench my fists and lay them on my knees, facing up towards the darkened sky. It is almost like the weather has stopped to look at me like I usually look upon it, deciding what I am and why I have accepted the elements' anger. The lightning is starting to form a shape. Surely that cannot be. My eyes are playing tricks on me. I stare in awe as I see it coil and compress into the form of a beautiful dragon. This beast is made entirely of electricity, yet I do not fear it as my common sense tells me I should. It is too beautiful to fear. It is too magical for it to be a force of evil. I feel that it has manifested itself into this form to please me, not cause me dismay.

The hairs on my arms start to prickle, and a clap of thunder breaks the silence. The dragon of light hovers and plays with the wind above, like a leaf blown from a tree in a heavy gust, it darts and glides, riding the winds as they flow. It stops directly above me, looking down at me and I up at it. It feels familiar, almost like it is family. A warmth envelops me, and I feel new, reborn even. I watch as everything around me seems to slow. Through the circle of clouds and rain, I watch as a bolt of lightning pours from the dragon's mouth towards my head. My mind tells me to panic, yet my heart is filled with a sense of complete tranquillity. My body is accepting the moment. The beauty and wonder of it revealing itself as a friend, not foe. The lightning, as if reaching down from the heavens, touches my forehead, and all I see is a burst of light. It was almost like it streamed from my own eyes and back into the sky above, meeting the dragon's breath with my own. My entire body starts tingling, feeling every small mist particle, every blade of grass touching my legs, and swirls of wind gently kissing my face. The elements and I are now an extension of each other, and they are calling to me. The feelings overwhelm me; I start to see darkness as my consciousness departs.

I wake, lying in a pool of brown muddy water, the sun has returned, and its gaze warms my face. Sitting up, I rub my eyes.

'How long was I asleep for?'
I stand, searching the skies for the storm. There is nothing but blue above me, bright and beautiful. I start to run, a feeling of power surges through my limbs, making me fleeter footed then I have ever been. The mud is no longer a problem. My feet feel grounded, and my balance is perfect as I race towards my home feeling fresher than I can remember.

'Father, Father!'

Out of nowhere, a flash of steel flies towards my head. I twist in mid-air, dodging the blade quickly. It lands in the ground, the tip of the sword in the dirt, hilt pointing towards me. I look up and see my father, an uncharacteristic frown on his face, brow wrinkled and drawn. He is wielding his beloved *Senso*.

'Father?'

'That is *Meiyo*, your sword son. Now defend yourself.'

Meiyo, a sword named after honour and glory, a blade of my own!

He launches himself forward, preparing an attack. I grab at *Meiyo* quickly and get into a defensive stance. It feels so delicate in comparison to my wooden blade. I almost forget myself observing how beautiful the sword is — a dragon engraved on the edge with the symbol for honour carved into the handle. Remembering my father's attack, I lift my new sword to parry his strike. He is ruthless and furiously swings at me. What seemed like a dance to me before now makes my father as fierce as the grim reaper himself. My father looks like a different person. These are not the kata that I have been learning in training, but strikes designed for death.

'Father, stop!'

'I will stop when you defeat me.' he screams as I see him ready for another attack.

My father charges towards me, leaving himself open. I crouch and spin on a single knee as *Senseo* flies just inches above my head. I strike at the back of my father's knees with a tilted blade so that my sword's blunt edge hits and therefore causing no damage. Father drops to the floor, and I stand, blade ready in case he leaps into another attack. He rises slowly, turning back to face me with a massive smile on his face. Suddenly father starts to chant, in the same way I remember from many years ago. His skin begins to glow, and with a flash of light, he is gone. Suddenly, I feel a blade against my throat.

'How did you do that?' I ask, shocked.

'You can do it too, Son, I have seen it in you. I recognised that storm today. I once sat in it like you.'

'You knew this would happen?'

'It is our gift, and it is time for you to learn more about our ability to control the elements. You are awakened.'

Chapter Five – Elements Sun

Training changed dramatically for me. The once tiring aspects grow much more comfortable — the focus shifts to elemental control.

'Although this training is the most important aspect of your journey, do not forget about the basics you have been practising. If you are inside, you will not have control over the weathers,' my father explains.

I nod to let him know I understand. We begin with lessons on how to feel the weather. Strange as it is; They are suddenly a part of me, an extension of my being, something that has always been there. It has been such a massive part of my life, and only now do I realise why. This secret kept by both my parents, aware that it would manifest, yet telling me nothing.

'Focus, Jacob, the sun is out, feel it on your skin, absorb the power. It will be subtle; you won't be overwhelmed by it, and you must not fear the strange sense of it.'

I close my eyes and feel the warmth of the morning sun on my skin, reminding me of the time in my room, attempting to replicate my father's song. Does this mean I did see him float? The feeling I get is not as subtle as my father has suggested. The heat hits me like a tsunami of energy, and although it is a beautifully hot day, I feel the hairs all over my body rise. They reach towards the power, almost clawing at it, begging for the sun to allow it's energy to be tamed. I start to glow.

'Jacob! This is amazing, never have I ever...' My father looks at me with excitement and shock.

I open my eyes, feeling like I imagine a god would. The power inside me is churning. It twists, wanting to be released, yet healing my aches and making me feel invincible.

'Run Jacob, use the power run to the other side of the field and back,' my father shouts.

I look towards the edge of the farm. It must be a good two acres away. Taking a deep breath, I launch myself forward. I accelerate at such a speed that I leave my stomach and senses behind me. My feet barely touch the ground as I flash forward towards my goal. The wind blasting my face, and I struggle to keep my eyes open. The trees I pass are nothing but a blur. Suddenly, I fall. I fly 20 feet and hit the ground rolling through mud and grass, feeling a sharp pain rise through my thighs.

'What the hell happened?' I ask in a daze.

My father, in another flash of light, rushes over to me.

'You will need to think more about your environment, Jacob.'

'What happened, father?'

'Well, look back over there,'

I look back towards my path, realising that I had run straight through the fence on the edge of the farm.

'Moving at that speed can be tough on the eyes, but if you don't look where you are going, it can be tough on your whole body. Be thankful that it was just a fence and not a building.' My father starts to laugh.

'Don't make me laugh; it hurts.'

'Here is lesson two. The sun is a healer. Focus again on absorbing the power from it, then focus on where the pain is.'

I sit up, covered in mud and once again start to absorb the power of the sun. I feel my body repairing itself, the abrasions on my thighs close in front of my eyes, knitting together and scabbing over in seconds. In a few moments, the scab falls off and is replaced with perfectly smooth and untouched skin.

'How many times have you done that after a battle? I always thought that you never got hit.'

'I never do get hit, but I have damaged myself training. The power you now have can be dangerous, which is why we must follow the bushido path and never use them to hurt the innocent. Now son, tell me. Which of the seven codes of bushido are the most important to you?'

'Jin, compassion. Makato, honesty and sincerity and finally Meiyo, honour.'

'A good choice, son. Never forget these in times of turmoil. Life will try to beat them out of you, so you must be strong, and you must be in control. Remember, never use these gifts to harm unless you have no choice. Rise above petty conflict and instead, use them to protect those who need it most.'

I smile to myself; my father is a hero. He wields all this power yet has remained a sensitive and kind man.

'I hope... I hope I do you proud father,'

My father hugs me, holding the grasp for a few moments. He releases me and points back to the farmhouse, 'Now run back, use the power but be aware of your surroundings, and please do not break anything else.'

I focus on my destination; my body alights with power and warmth. I take another deep breath and in a flash, am back at the farmhouse. I hear my father's cheers from afar.

I start using the power for everything. Flashing out of my room for breakfast, I zip around while tending the farm. I hammer in fence posts at super speed and spend the next few weeks running in every direction, learning to avoid the rocks, boulders, trees and animals in my path. Unfortunately, the rest of the world continues at average speed. Time does not slow when I move fast, my reactions can still let me down in combat, so I spar with father and mother every day.

Learning how to use subtle movement in the art of fighting is more complicated than running around doing things. The actions are so minor that the slightest mistake can cause me to slice my father in two with overextending a sword thrust. I could end up punching through my opponent's body when using hand to hand fighting techniques. I need to be very careful.

I gradually improve, pushing myself in my usual manner, that same manner that will make me great. Father often forces me to fight without the use of powers, making sure that I will still be able to protect myself when I fight inside. I admit to not enjoying this side of combat as much. I do, however, love the feeling that the power gives me, the sheer strength and movement capabilities, and you can get everything done considerably faster especially chores.

'Father, why have you never shown these powers to me before, and why could I never tell when you were in a duel?'

'If people knew about this, would they not be jealous? Would they not see it as an unfair advantage?'

'Yes, I suppose they would, but wouldn't they just leave you alone then?'

'No, they would not. Instead, hordes of warriors would try to get rid of me, and no doubt you and your mother too. People always want what they can't have, and people always fear what they do not understand.'

I ponder his words, but for once, I struggle to understand. Surely if people knew of the power they had, they would fear them too much to fight? Then I realise, my father had told me before, to be feared is to be a tyrant. My father hides his power so that people would not fear him. He would rather only fight when he has to, using the energy to protect, not to kill for the sake of killing, or just because he has the power to do so.

My control of the sun seems to peak. The sensations become as much a part of me as breathing — the warming, healing heat of it, natural. I focus on its power, and it seems to oblige me by focusing on me in return, allowing every pore in my flesh absorb it, the power manifesting within my body. Flash running becomes far easier; I learn how to use it subtly, releasing minor amounts to speed my movements. Sword swings, kicks and punches are fast, but I make sure they are not too fast. My mental perception of these movements is still considerably slower than my body's speed; my father assures me that it will stay like that forever. My mind struggling to keep up.

Yielding this power does have its downfalls, however. If an overzealous punch or kick strikes an opponent without first releasing the energy of speed and converting it to strength, I may shatter my bones and be left having to heal. It can take hours, even in direct sunlight. A broken bone in combat is less than ideal.

Chapter Six – Elements Wind

'The wind is a very different element to control. It swerves and moves in what seems like an inconsistent manner,' my father explains. He then starts to move, one movement flowing to another, shifting and dancing in patterns. I watch as my father gracefully manoeuvres his body in a sword kata. The wind starts to follow him, swirling about his body; father starts playing with the winds around him, like small tornados whirling on his arms. I stand in admiration. He switches stance and pushes out with his arms. The mini tornados shift from his forearms and fire forward in a gust, producing a force that could easily knock a man off his feet.

'Wow! That was amazing, father.'

'The winds are the hardest to capture, but once you have mastered them...'
Father starts to run; the winds start swirling around his legs, suddenly he jumps, yet not a
normal jump nor a human jump; he flips, spinning through the air and lands on the roof of the house.

'Haha!' I excitedly chuckle to myself.

'Your turn.'

I start to sense the wind blowing around me, the air alive with movement. I close my eyes and feel out the flurries of air. I attempt to move with them, realising that they are not random at all. They move consistently, running in circles, playing with their surroundings, bending the grass, bouncing off walls, almost like a small child exploring an environment for the first time. My arms start to shift and swirl. The wind seems to notice and becomes drawn to me. I observe them around me as they caress my arms, drift through my hair and delicately stroke my face. I turn and move, feeling light as a feather. I start running and jumping around our farm fields, making sense of this very different power. The sun made me feel powerful and safe, but this is new and fresh. I get a feeling of total freedom. I feel like a child again. I jump up to join my father, the force lifting me a little too far and clear the entire house. Twenty feet above my home, I start to descend. Panic dawns on me as I hurtle towards the floor. I hit it hard, rolling over and feel something crunch in my side.

'Are you ok?' Ezekiel asks, rushing over to me.

'I think I cracked a rib.'

'Well, what are you going to do about it, son?'

I pause, focusing on the sun, drawing in its healing power. I feel the swelling in my ribs subside as it returns to its original state. It seemed to heal faster this time, like my body is getting used to absorbing the sun for healing. Could that be true? Or was the injury less than my previous ones?

'Ok, I'm better. Let's try some more.'

My father smiles and darts off. 'Catch me if you can!'

I stand, my side feeling nothing of the injury it just sustained, and race after my father. Asking the winds for help, I shift and turn as my father leaps over objects and runs along posts and fences, objects much smaller than the house this time. I attempt to emulate him. I do an excellent job of keeping up, but I am still the clumsy shadow of my father. I watch him approach the river, racing as fast as he can, the wind pushing him forward. As he reaches the bank, he shifts the swirls to his feet. I watch as they snake down his body and fixate themselves to the undersides of his shoes. He races over the water, the winds carrying him across as if it were solid underfoot, not a river of shifting torrents. I stop at the edge.

'Hey! That's cheating,' I shout. Father bows to me. I think I know how he did that. I need more than just the air to walk on water. I start to absorb the sun, feeling the power to flash forward and at the same time calling to the winds to allow me to hover. Father watches from the other side of the river. A worried look appears on his face as his mouth widens. Father waves his arms from across the river, taunting me, I guess, so I persist. He tries to shout, goading me on to get to him. As I start to run, something feels very wrong. The sun and winds are clashing, much like the beginning of a storm. I feel a sudden surge of tension in the air. The weathers explode in a furore of heat and wind. I am thrown through the air, twisting out of control. The wind takes hold of me and pulls me back towards the river; I land safely but with a splash, softening my landing. I must have reached thirty-foot high in that explosion. As I surface, my father is sitting on the river bank, waving me to swim across. I paddle over and take a seat beside him.

'I am sorry, son. I had not prewarned you that mixing the elements is problematic and somewhat... explosive.'

'No one got hurt father, so please don't fret,' I smile.

'I have never quite understood the reasons for it. I guess that's why storms can be so devastating. The weathers fight above us, the battle causing lightning, high winds and floods. Yet, one cannot live without the other.'

'I understand.'

'Ok, let's try that again.'

I leap to my feet, eager to impress this time and hopefully have a less soggy ending.

'Control the air first. Always control then act.'

'Okay, father.' I start to feel the winds coil around my body; it is almost snake-like, wrapping itself around my limbs as it did my father before he walked on water. I feel it moving down from my body to my legs. For a moment, I feel like I am about to walk the plank of a pirate ship. I step towards the water's edge, looking straight down into the river I had become friends with just moments before. I step forward, somewhat sheepishly, into what could be another wet end. The winds have other ideas. They playfully waltz with the surface of the river, teasing and caressing it and holding firm just a few inches off the top of the water. I walk across the surface, unstable and off-balance, but a walk nonetheless. I reach the other side in the manner of a baby taking his first stumbles.

'Well done,' my father exclaims proudly.

'Thank you, father. I hope I get better at that. The jumping part is easy, but sauntering, not so much.'

I practice till nightfall. Getting wet a few more times, but eventually, it all seems to come together. I find it easier to sprint across the surface than to walk. Whoever said you must learn to walk before you can run was not an Elementalist.

'Son, wake up.'

'Is everything ok, father?'

'Yes, everything is fine. We have an early start for today's lesson.'

I peer out of my window to see the sun has not awoken itself yet. I take my tired body out of bed and dress. We take a short moment to eat breakfast; my mother is still in bed, so breakfast is adequate but not as delicious as her creations.

'Why are we training in the dark?'

'All will be revealed soon,' my father explains as we polish off our morning meal.

We spend a few more minutes waiting for food to go down and make our way out. I pick up my sword on the way through, but my father stops me. 'You won't need that today.'

'Are we not training?'

'We are, but this training is different, so put down your blade and come out into the darkness with me.'

I place my sword back on its stand, glancing once again at its beauty, its magnificence and the ivory hilt with one simple Japanese symbol etched into it. Meiyo. I run over to my father.

'Son, the air around us is a constant swirl of energy and power. There will be some days with no rain, some with no sun, but never does a day go by without a breeze, even of the slight kind. It shifts, it turns, it crashes, and it sails. Once you embrace that power, you will feel like you can fly, not just walk on water. There is another power that the wind holds. It carries things. Do you know what it carries?'

I contemplate the riddle, what can air carry? Leaves? No. Dirt? No. 'I have got no idea, father.'

'Sound,' he states. 'It carries sounds, many of them. Be it the crash of rocks, the swaying of branches or even perhaps the voice of a man or growl of a beast.'

'Of course, now I understand.'

'Allow yourself to get lost in the darkness son, and remain as silent as a mountain. Allow your ears to accept the power and tell you stories from beyond our sight.'

I close my eyes. All I hear are gusts, but soon those gusts start to make sense. Fragments of information begin to piece together into familiar sounds. I listen as the wind crashes over the great tree in our field. I hear the bleating of sheep that are waking. 'It is working, father.'

'I am going to disappear across the field son; you will not see me, but if you concentrate, you will hear me. I shall send you a message from over there. Let's see if you can understand it,' and with that, he walks away from the minimal light peeking out of the windows of our house and into the darkness. His form melts away, from man to shadow, to nothing. I continue trying to hear what the wind is carrying. It picks up my father's steps, the breeze suggesting that he is purposefully stealthy. Suddenly, in a swirl of noises, his actions disappear. I would guess that he has used the wind to travel silently across the pathway.

The noises start to change. I hear a voice in the air, but it is different from the sound of someone shouting. It's far more subtle. The whispers on the wind make my ears tingle - they flow to me, telling me the stories that are carried around within the twists and swirls. A voice I recognise appears to me. 'If you hear me, throw your voice my way.'

'I hear you, father, I say softly, attempting to hide my voice as much as I can.

'A softly spoken word still travels on the wind like any other,' he responds.

The rest of the morning is made up of conversations on the wind. We move away from using our voices and venture forth to different parts of the village. We listen to the townsfolk without their realisation. Learn some secrets, have some laughs, like the fact Ol' Roger has a terrible wart, in a rather untoward place that he calls Dennis, and I learn how difficult it is to separate one voice from another. After a few days, however, I get the hang of it. It takes less time to piece together the fragments of noise and becomes easier to decipher them. The awakening has gifted me these powers, which strangely feel like they have always been a part of me, coming to me as naturally as walking, sometimes even breathing.

Chapter Seven – Elements Rain

'The effects of the rain are far subtler than that of the sun and wind. Controlling it feels different, yet when you focus on it… try it for yourself, son. Go and sit out in the downpour, let it overwhelm you, feel every droplet of rain that strikes you,' my father says.

I nod to my father and walk out of the house and into the blanket of greywater. It falls heavily from the sky, quickly drenching my clothing. Each drop is poking and prodding its icy fingers on the bare parts of my body. My face, hands and feet are feeling the chill from its cold touch. Despite all this, it feels comfortable; it almost feels familiar. I compare the streaks of water upon my face to the gentle touch of my mother, only much cooler - the way she used to soothe my pain or anguish as a child with a tender stroke of my cheek. A homely comfort, one that does not judge and does not expect, it's just is how it should be.

The water pours into my eyes, forcing them shut. I start to think about the water surrounding me. The puddles have been accumulating since the rain began this morning. They are making the paddocks look more like rice fields. There is so much water that this should be an easy task. While I sit, soaking and cold, I reach out for the water that surrounds me, yet cannot feel anything but the numbness that has started to mask my body.

'Nothing is happening, Father!.'

I hear my father approach, sitting by my side.

'What are you focusing on, son?'

'The water that surrounds us. The puddles, there is so much of it, why can't I feel anything?'

'You can only focus on the elements that have been gifted by the heavens, son. As soon as the water strikes the earth, they become of the earth.'

'Why?'

'Son, for now, focus on the rain, the drops that have journeyed from above us, those life-giving gifts.'

I turn to look at my father, sitting just a few feet away from me, yet not a drop of rain touches him. He glances back at me, giving me a mischievous smirk, 'Still getting wet?' suddenly, his expression changes. 'Do you hear that?' he asks.

In a sudden flurry of movements, I see the rain shift in front of him as an arrow misses his head by mere inches. The broad missile strikes the ground behind us. It is at least two full arm lengths tall. Feathers caress its behind, painted red, white and black. Its metallic arrowhead is driven far into the earth, disguising its exact size. The bow that fired this arrow must be that of a giant. My father launches himself off the ground, unsheathing *Senso* and stooping into a guard position. I have left my blade in the house, so I run for cover in the doorway, gazing out into the dullness beyond for any sign of an enemy hidden in the dark grey that surrounds us. I listen to the wind, searching for signs of movement. The rain overwhelms most of the noise that usually surrounds us. I hear a faint burst of displacement as if something is pushing the wind and rain from its path. My father is quick to react, and with a flash of his blade and a nimble sidestep, he strikes the second arrow from the sky.

'You are as good as they say, Neph,' an unfamiliar voice speaks.

Out of the gloom, a silhouette as large as a barn door yet in the shape of a man appears. 'Please, be at ease. I shall refrain from wasting any more arrows on you.'

'Have you come to challenge me?' My father asks politely.

'I have not. I simply wanted to see if the rumours about your skills were true, and I am not disappointed.'

The man advances closer to my father. His features start to birth from the curtain of rain that envelops us. The man's shoulders are broad enough to tackle a charging bison. A pointed straw hat casts a shadow upon his face, hiding his eyes but leaving his wry smile in full view. He wears a cloak of green and brown, sewn together chaotically, seemingly to replicate the scattering of leaves or greenery and bush composition. I feel that if this man didn't want us to see him, we wouldn't.

'I am glad to have not disappointed,' my father bows toward the man.

'I should not have attacked you unawares. There is no honour in such actions.'

'My name is Ezekiel; do you have a name marksman?'

'I am Bipin.'

'Welcome, friend, have you travelled far to be here?'

'Very.'

'Then please accept the hospitality of my house and home, let us save any future combat for a day we are both equally refreshed.'

'I have no intention of entering into combat with you, sir.'

'Be that as it may, you have travelled far and for more than the firing of a few arrows at me, no?'

The man named Bipin nods in agreement, 'Thank you, I accept your hospitality.'

I carefully watch the stranger as he enters our home. He removes his hat to release his long, black locks of hair adorning a single white and gold eagle feather. His skin is far darker than ours, and his eyes reveal deep-rooted wisdom matched with that of a seasoned hunter and a bright shade of turquoise. They almost shine, like the flames of candles painted by the ocean. I remain unsure of what this man would hunt.

He is tremendous in stature, yet, despite his intimidating frame, he wanted to stay hidden from us and did an excellent job of it.

'May I take your cloak?' My father asks.

'Thank you,' says Bipin, removing his camouflage cape. Hiding underneath is a cuirass of hardened leather. Burnt into the front is another eagle. Its wings are spreading across his breast, the tips touching the warrior's shoulders. Stemming from them are arms lean and muscular, the sort that could fire missiles from a bow built for giants.

Bipin notices me eyeing him, 'Fear not, I am no enemy of yours.' His eyes are fixated on me, and I feel he is learning all he can about me through his gaze. I feel a calming sensation envelop me.

My mother glides over in her usual graceful manner, wielding a tray of steaming tea for us. Bipin rises when he spots her, bowing graciously to thank her for the warming beverage. She smiles in acceptance. When I watch her soft touch and its effect on people, I forget how fierce a warrior she is. I have only sparred with her once, but it was enough to understand that she and my father are equals in combat.

'Thank you, Telaá,' my father says.

'You are most welcome,' she says, smiling warmly. She sits next to my father and slides her hand upon his.

'I am a watcher, Ezekiel,' the stranger states.

My father's eyes widen, and an unusually hard look appears on his face. My mother's soft features turn into a scowl; this is the first time I have ever seen her like this. 'You will have to kill us both before you get anywhere near my son,' my mother hisses.

'I am not here for that reason, Telaá. You have been summoned.'

'You must know that we cannot go?' my father states.

'It is your burden; it is your place.'

'It stopped being our burden when you all turned your back on us, Watcher.'

'Times of need are upon us. Bring your son; I have searched his soul, he is more good than... than the alternative.'

'We made sure of that Bipin. We are good folk, and we know how to bring up our only son,' my mother argues.

'What's is going on?' I plead, feeling lost in a whirlpool of conversation.

'I promise to explain fully soon, son,' my father responds. 'You have our answer Bipin, and we appreciate the time it must have taken to get here, but we will not change our stance.'

'Very well, Neph.'

What is Neph?

'I respect your decision and take my leave. Thank you for your hospitality, and thank you for the excellent tea, Telaá. I must warn you, you may take leave of your responsibilities, and I understand why. Your forbidden engagement could have caused the end. Yet, I can see that the boy is nothing of what the prophecy stated. He is why we want you to return. Darkness looms in the far ends of the earth, one that threatens us all.'

'A darkness?' my father responds.

'Yes, the six have been called upon, yet only three have returned.'

'Where are the two remaining warriors?'

'Dead perhaps? Hence why the watchers have been summoned,' says the mountain of a man.

My mother and father look at each other, their usual calm demeanour replaced by that of worry.

'What shall we do, my love?' My mother grasps my father's hand tight.

'I will not risk our son for the sake of a stupid prophecy. He is too important.'

'But what if it is true?'

'They told us that our love would be the start of another end time, but look,' my father gazes at me with the love only a father can give. 'He is perfect, caring, considerate, everything we made sure he was.'

'I will leave you to decide. Know this. Even if you do not answer the call, you will have to fight sooner or later.' The warrior bows to the three of us, lingering for a few extra moments on me, his searching eyes gazing into mine, looking for answers to questions I don't know.

Bipin lifts his cloak and throws it over his head. He coils his long locks of hair up, placing his hat on top of his head, and makes for the door. He pauses for a moment, his giant silhouette almost filling the frame of the doorway. He turns and looks to me again, 'Till we meet again, Jacob.' He bows and steps out into the waiting weather, disappearing into the bleakness almost instantly.

'What is going on?' I ask my parents.

Chapter Eight – The Death of a Legend

I wake to the sound of light rain. The pattering on my wooden walls has become friendlier since my awakening. I stretch, rousing my body and prising myself out of my comfortable bed. I walk to my shuttered window, pushing it open and allowing the waking sunlight to pour in. The weather hasn't yet decided what today will hold for the sky. Rain and sun, still dancing with each other as the morning rises. To me, there is no good or bad weather anymore; there are only different abilities that come with each. Do I move in flashes to achieve my goals, or do I control the rain and learn more about how I can utilise it in combat? Do I listen to the whispers on the wind, or do I fight with sword and fist? The weather dictates my training now. It is my friend, my sparring partner and my teacher. I feel sorry for those that do not feel what I feel.

The wind's whisper drifts through my open window, warning me that someone approaches the house. In the kitchen, my parents sit around the oak table. The familiar smells of breakfast are nonexistent this morning. A well dressed man bows to my parents and leaves the house. I see my mother with her arms around my father, pulling him in close to her. His eyes are red, and I see the pathways of tears on his cheek. I have never seen my father cry, nor my mother looking solemn. For the first time in my life, my father looks vulnerable, almost aged, compared to yesterday.

'Is everything ok?'

'Ezekiel's sword master has died,' my mother replies.

I have never heard him mention his master. I have always pictured my father as being born the warrior he is today. I step in front of him, bowing in respect. 'I am sorry for your loss, Father.'

Looking up to meet my eyes for the first time since I entered the room, 'Thank you, Son'

It feels alien to me to see my father sad.

'Come,' he says, 'Let us take a walk.' He reluctantly stands, and my mother seems to grasp him tighter. He looks at her and nods gently. 'It is time he knew, my love.' She releases him from her grasp, and he exits the house. I take a moment to smile at my mother then follow suit, leaving the house to catch up with my father.

The heat of the rising sun forces its way into my skin. I naturally absorb it now; it makes me feel powerful almost instantly. I know my father feels the same, but it would seem that not even its warm touch can lift his spirit on this day. We continue to walk in silence for what seems like miles. I say nothing, waiting for my father to be ready to open up to me. I can sense that he is searching for the right words and explanations. His eyes are looking to the floor, and his brow furrowed. The silence breaks. 'Son, I have never mentioned my master, and I am sorry for that.' I nod in return, not knowing if he can see my reactions. 'In my younger days, I was unwise. I did not listen to all of the teachings of my master; it is my greatest regret, but also, my greatest achievement.'

'Why is that, father?'

'You must understand, it is not the disagreement with him that I regret. If I had obeyed his requests, you would have never been born.'

'Thank you, father.'

'Thank you?'

'Yes. For if it weren't for your defiance, I wouldn't be here.'

'It was the last time we spoke, son. I left his teachings to marry your mother. He warned me that if we were together and bore children, then... then it could be catastrophic. We were told that if two Nephilim bore a child, it could become a dark angel. An angel of pure power and hate. I feel we have done a good job of ensuring you are pure of heart, my son. You are so strong, wise, and a true light, you couldn't possibly become what they believed you would.'

'Father, what is a Nephilim?'

'We are the sons and daughters of gods, my boy – the children of angels. That is why we have these powers. We are here to protect man from destroying itself like it once did. Your mother and I ran away together when we fell in love. We didn't want the responsibilities forced upon us. We wanted a family. We wanted you.'

'So a dark angel is evil but holds powers like ours?'

'Yes, the dark angel was banished for causing the final great war that almost destroyed all that remains of man. He made man selfish, greedy, materialistic and angry. Its influence was terrible, and his corruption bore its way into the minds of many.'

'How did he do that? With magic like ours?'

'No, with influence. Before the war, technology was immense. Small devices projected images all over the world, and he used those images to turn the world against each other. After the last great war, two-thousand years ago, he disappeared, fought off by the remaining six Nephilim.'

'So are you two-thousand years old?'

My father laughs, 'No, Son, I am not. Do I look two-thousand years old?'

'Of course not, but I do not yet know the limitations of our powers.'

'When one of us dies, our spirit glides into another host, born at the same time as the Nephilims death.'

'But I was born from you and mother, so am I a Nephilim?'

'Your powers show that you are, despite you being created more… traditionally. We had no idea what would happen, but we risked it anyway. We are thrilled we did. You are my everything, Son.'

'So you and mother didn't meet duelling?'

'We duelled a lot, Jacob. But we were called upon to the Nephilim temple to report to the others. We had a duel and fell in love. She is the fastest and most magnificent warrior I had ever met. Yet with a soul so gentle…'

I hear a loud noise from the mountains ahead. 'What was that?' I turn to look at my father, and the wind whizzes past my face, faster than anything I have felt. A splatter of wetness hits my cheek as the projectile connects with its target. It hits him so hard that his entire body flies backwards and lands on the floor like a lifeless ragdoll. I race over to my father's now soulless body, dropping to my knees, not understanding what has just happened. I am paralysed except for the uncontrollable shake that has overwhelmed me. I stare at my father as blood pours from his head and onto the grass surrounding us. My hero, my master, gone. A feeling of rage and pain overcomes me. Grief is forced aside. The sky above me turns grey and then black. Thunder booms above me as if shouting my father's name. My fingers draw blood from my palm. My fists clenched so tight my knuckles turn white. How could this happen? I scream towards the heavens, the wind shrieks in return, sharing this moment of despair with me as a sibling would.

'How could you allow this to happen! How could you let this perfect man die?' The heavens respond as lightning strikes the ground. The earth around me cracks with its ferocity. The lightening above swirls in anger, shifting unnaturally in the sky above. Then it forms like it did on the day of my awakening; The dragon, only this time it is not calm, it is not quiet - it breathes bolts of fury into the heavens. It is not the beautiful beast gliding around me that I witnessed before. It wants revenge, and I can feel it. This glorious beast mirrors my own emotion as if we are variations of the same soul temporarily separated. The ground shudders again as the elements battle above me. The rain evaporates as it strikes the dragon, the wind using its full force to try and knock it out of the sky, yet it persists in its furore.

The weather calms, understanding that the dragon of lightning cannot be matched in battle and cannot be expelled from the sky; instead, it embraces its presence. I once again feel the elements eyes upon me. It goes quiet. The dragon swirls and changes shape, shifting its body of light and power. It morphs into a silhouette of a human, my silhouette! It is now that I realise the dragon has always been me. It stares into my soul; it is the reflection of the man I can become. Its eyes are filling with pain, screaming in anger, it's body tense and wild. The killer I see is me.

The wind and rain leave, the clouds melt away, turning the sky back to the ocean hues after the sun ended its waltz with the rain, and I am left in a field, soaking.

'Father! Father, please!' I crouch before his body.

The tears are racing down my face. I hold my father's body against my legs, the remains of his head spewing out on the ground as I move him. I cannot look. What sort of evil could have killed the greatest warrior so easily and in such a manner? I glance towards the mountain.

'I will be back, father.' I place his body on the ground. I instantly start to absorb the sun. I see smoke coming from where the sound originated, and so flash move towards it. My anger fuels my speed, and I move at such velocity that the trees I pass are nothing more than a blur of green and brown.

In a flash, I arrive in the forest. The burning trees around me show that the killer wanted to cover their trail. This fire will grow if I don't do anything. There is no rain; the sky is clear and bright, and the sun blazes above me. It will take an age to put this out, and all the time, my father's body grows colder. What will my mother do when she finds out?

'Mother!' I look towards my homestead, more smoke, more fire, I cannot lose them both. I leave the forest to burn, flashing towards my home. I find my mother lying in the dirt.

'Still breathing, thank the gods!'

Her eyes open slowly. 'Jacob?'

'Yes mother, it is I. What happened here? Are you ok? Did anyone harm you?'

'Men came, but before I could defend myself, they spiked me with this,' she holds up a small feathered dart. 'After that, I passed out, the house was on fire, and you were holding me.'

'*Senso*, I must get it before the flames engulf everything.' I sit my mother up and race into the flame ridden house. The fire coils around the walls of my home. Snake-like wisps of heat caress the wood, urging it to blacken and burn. The heat becomes unbearable, and I am forced back out into the garden. *Senso* is nowhere to be seen, taken by the man who did this.

'Where is your father?'

'I'm sorry, mother, I couldn't save him,' a fresh tsunami of tears flood my eyes.

'Jacob?.'

'I'm sorry.'

'What happened? Did someone defeat him?'

'No, something hit him from the mountains. I have no idea what. It was not a bow but some kind of magic missile from over a mile away. It struck father in the head, and... and it killed him instantly.'

'What could have done such a thing?'

'I have no idea, mother, but I vow to find the person responsible.'

We both sit on the hard ground for what feels like days, feeling the heat from our burning home on our faces, witnessing our lives being destroyed. How could this have happened so suddenly? How was my father murdered so easily? Why was I not fast enough to save him? Not even the burning flames can dry our tears, and not even a blazing sun can heal these wounds. Only revenge can do that.

Chapter Nine – The Price of Death

I watch the pyre go up in flames, my father's body
upon it. My mother wields the torch; her body is
trembling despite her brave face. The flames wrap
around his covered body. A samurai mask covers
what is left of his kind features and soft eyes. The
mask itself, a masterful carving of wood. A dragon's
head with a sun carved on the forehead. It was at my
mother's request; the sun had always been the
element that felt like home to father.

I have no idea who could have done this. My
father's senses and speed were faster than anything I
could ever imagine. He sometimes seemed faster than
the winds themselves. What could have finished him
so easily?

My mother weeps softly. Her youthful smile
and bright eyes darkened, the grief almost too much
for her. I glance at the gathered crowd. Fellow
farmers from the town have come to pay their
respects to the fallen master. Even their eyes are red,
stained with the grief we all share. They have come

with gifts of food, livestock and offers to help rebuild our home. They are good people.

The flames grow high and fierce as they stretch out to touch the sky. The wood crackles and breaks down as it burns my father's remains. Smoke and stench bellow out of it, not even the incense placed within the wooden frames of the pyre can hide the smell of burning flesh; I feel sick.

The town monk gestures for my mother to speak. 'Do you wish to say anything, Telaá?'

'Okay.'

I hadn't noticed him speaking until now. I had been staring into the fire, reminiscing moments lost. My mother steps to the front of the crowd, turning to face them. 'He…' She waivers slightly, her sobs threatening to overwhelm her. I take my place by her side, holding her hand and hoping to bring her strength. 'He was our hero.'

Fresh tears scramble from her eyes. 'Perfect,' I whisper to her. Those four simple words are enough. He was a hero to all of us. A hero that protected us all, a hero that fought so others didn't have to, a hero that deserved more than this end. I feel her body shake with each inhalation, the warrior within her fighting to stow the remaining grief. Her usual flawless features look tired and withdrawn, as if her spirit has left her body to chase my father's as it ascends to the heavens.

'Don't let this change you, Mother. Don't let the price of death be so substantial as to take your life too.' Her pale eyes look to mine, searching for something, perhaps an image of my father? Perhaps a show of hope. 'Mother…' I am cut off by the monk finishing his speech. They had no idea who my father was. I feel a pang of rage building within me, a wave of fury surrounding my body.

'I must find out who did this,' I say to my mother.

'Yes, you must, Son.'

I notice a familiar figure emerging from the shadows of the trees opposite. 'Mother, Bipin is here.' I feel the urge to flash over to that mountainous watcher and start demanding answers. I cannot give my power away, not even to these friends that surround us.

'Perhaps he is here to pay his respects?'

'Perhaps.'

Bipin nods at me, an acknowledgement of my spotting him on the horizon. I do believe, however, if that man didn't want to be seen, he would be invisible. How does he do that?

As the ceremony finishes, every person attending walks by my mother and me, offering condolences. We accept them graciously, yet all I can think about is why Bipin is here. Thankfully, I am not left waiting long; he lingers on the doorstep as we get back to our partially rebuilt home.

'Greetings again, young Jacob and Telaá. I am very sorry to hear about the passing of Ezekiel.'

'Passing? You mean murder,' I say.

'Apologies,' Bipin bows his head.

'Jacob, please stop. This is not Bipin's fault. Let us go inside.'

As we enter, the smell of burning is still prominent. The house seems to have absorbed the stench of fire and death. It does not feel familiar anymore. Its changes are subtle, like the shadows that favour the corners of the sun-starved room, are darker than usual.

'Tea?' my mother asks.

'Please, allow me,' responds Bipin. He replaces her in the kitchen, crushing a flower unknown to me. Its dark purple leaves are crumbling in the hands of the giant man.

After a few minutes, he returns to us, placing a hot goblet of tea on the table.

'This will help,' he says.

I watch my mother take a sip. A slight smile touches her lips, one I thought was lost forever. The smile reminds me of how beautiful and elegant she was before my father's murder. I quaff the drink, and an overwhelming feeling of warmth surrounds me. Not the sort from drinking something hot, but more like the embrace of a parent or sibling. For the first time since his death, I feel my rage dissipate, and a feeling of calm surrounds me. Whatever this stuff is, it is beautiful.

'I come with news that may be of interest to you.,' says Bipin. 'It regards your father's killer.'

'Spill it then, Bipin,' I say.

'You must not allow your rage to control you, young one, not yet at least.'

'Fine. I will do what I can.'

'Not good enough. You must vow it.'

'Okay, I vow to remain calm, although I'm pretty sure this tea will make sure of that.'

Bipin pauses for a moment, peering into me as the watcher always does, gaze fixated on my eyes, looking for the truth in them.

'Very well. The man you seek is known as the Archivist. I cannot tell you exactly which domain he resides in, but I can tell you that most of his business seems to be within the walls of Neodeas, the metropolis.'

'How do you know this?' my mother asks.

'I am a watcher; it is my business to see the great wonders and disturbances of this world.'

'So, when do we leave?' I ask the watcher.

'Unfortunately, I cannot interfere in the workings of humans.'

'You look pretty human to me? Large, but human.'

'Jacob, I am a watcher. That is different.'

'Did you watch my father's death?'

'As I said, we are not allowed to interfere.'

'So that is a yes. You watched while my father was murdered.'

'Please, Jacob, I am not of this realm. I cannot be a part of it. Our code forbids such action against a human.'

'Fuck your code, watcher.'

'Jacob!' my mother shouts. 'You will stop talking to Bipin in that manner immediately.'

I suddenly realise I am standing, hand on the hilt of my sword.

'Apologies, apologies to you both. I made a vow,' I bow my head to Bipin.

'I understand your pain, Jacob. This Archivist must be stopped. The artefacts he holds are too dangerous and must be destroyed.'

'Why are you telling my son this?'

'Because it is his task, Telaá.'

'He can't go; he has never left the farm region.'

'If he does not go, we all lose.'

'Mother, please. I will go, give me some time to gather my things. Tell me more about this Neodeas.'

Chapter Ten – Kindred Spirits

I pack light on the advice of Bipin. The journey will be long, and flash travelling on unknown lands is dangerous. I could run into buildings, rocks, animals or even people. The scent of my mother's sticky rice floods into my room. She has packed the rice balls with berries. They keep well and are a great food to travel with, seeing they can easily be wrapped in cloth and won't rot for days.

I sheath my freshly sharpened blade, the sword gifted to me by my father, and make my way to the kitchen where my mother and Bipin await. He walks to me, his eagle gaze checking my armour and weapon. He pulls at the straps on the leather chest piece to make sure I have correctly fastened it.

'He is ready,' states Bipin.

'As much as I ever will be.' I give a fake smile to my mother, and she graciously returns it. Her eyes are drawn yet not wrinkling when she smiles back.

'You will need these,' she hands me the rice balls, wrapped and ready along with a few skins of water.

'Thank you, mother.'

'Remember your powers, son. They can be used for so much more than just fighting. Stay sharp and sleep lightly in the wilderness.'

'Will you be ok?' I ask, holding her face in my hands.

'I will be. Just focus on bringing back *Senso*. I am stronger than I look, Jacob.'

'I know you are. We have sparred on many occasions,' I say, this time giving a genuine smile.

I hug my mother and nod to Bipin. 'Here I go then,' I step out of the door and don't look back.

Three weeks of walking. The trees and animals that are native to my eyes have been left behind. I have not recognised the areas I am trudging for about a week now. My curiosity keeps me going. What is this metropolis going to be like? Bipin had tried to explain it to me, yet I am finding it difficult to imagine a forest of houses and humans. Smog blanketing the sky, making the whole world underneath seem darker, paired with the stench of an overpopulated city. Yes, city, that's what he called it. It's hard to imagine. Who would choose to live in that manner? Why wouldn't you want open fields and rivers so clean, you can drink from them? Where would they run or train?

'The humans there are much like a gathering of hyenas,' Bipin explained. 'Although, among them, some noble creatures still reside.'

I don't think he realised that I have no idea what a hyena is. The message, however, remains clear enough.

Within these three weeks, there has been nothing but sunshine relentlessly burning the ground. It is good for me in some ways; the sun heals my body, so I suffer no aches or pain. The constant healing power has meant that I have been able to cover a lot of ground quickly, reducing the time I need to sleep. My water supply, however, is running very low. The wilds are not a place that water is easy to come by. The ground is dry and arid. Even the grass is swaying less; its usual complexion of deep green now looks thirsty and brown.

'Come on rain, give me something,' I say while looking to the heavens.

As I continue walking, a slight breeze caresses me with a cooling touch. I enjoy a moment of respite as the hair on my skin prickles and reaches out to grab at the cooler air. I hold it close to my body, allowing it to surround me for a moment of stillness. The breeze also brings with it a whisper, telling me that another creature is close by. The almost silent padding of paw to floor gives away the large feline. I decide to take a closer look, but caution must be taken. These beasts can be ferocious, and I do not want to cause harm to a creature that is only trying to survive. It is not easy to sneak up on cats, so I ask the wind to help me. It obliges by wrapping itself around my feet, like tiny tornados, whisking me up an inch off the floor, making my movements almost silent. I hear a deep and rumbling growl. Poking my head out of the bristling reeds, I realise that this was once a river and a probable water source for all the animals that roam here. That water is gone. There is nothing but the dry reeds that have become my hiding spot and dusty, dry ground. I glance across the riverbed at what used to be a magnificent leopard. Its golden coat layered with a pattern of black spots, covering its emaciated body. It's beryl eyes are navigating the ground for water; it seems almost empty of hope. I didn't think it was possible to see this in such a grand wild thing.

I silently remove my pack, opening it as gently as possible. I take out my last two skins of water and last rice ball. Placing them on my pack, I shape the leather using stones to hold the water in place, much like a bowl. I open the skins and pour the water into it. Backing away slowly, I purposefully make noise, hopefully drawing the attention of the leopard.

After waiting for a few minutes, I realise the cat isn't coming.

'Hello, Hyo, HYO!...Where are you, beautiful beast?' I say to myself. I move back into my reeds, exploring the river. It doesn't take long to see it, lying on the floor, barely able to move.

'Oh, you poor thing. Don't worry. I can help you.' I rush back to my pack, gently lift it, and be careful not to spill the slightest bit of precious water. I lay it by the mouth of the creature. Its huge teeth peek out of an even bigger mouth. It just looks at me, not caring about my presence, just lying there, motionless.

'You will not die today, Hyo. Not with me here. So get up and drink this now.'

I pour a small amount of water into Hyo's mouth. For a few moments, nothing happens, but suddenly the leopard's tongue starts to move, lapping up the water. For the first time, Hyo shifts her entire body, placing her head closer to the pack and drinking the rest of the water.

'Here, friend,' I break off a piece of the rice ball and feed it to her. She graciously takes it and the rest of the food without hesitation. For a small moment, Hyo and I are kindred spirits, the beast and I both creatures trying to survive in this harsh land.

Gazing back up into the sky, I curse, 'Come on rain, how could you let this beautiful creature suffer? Give her water; else she will die in this dried up hell.'

Then it happens. I hear the most beautiful sound of thunder. Within a few minutes, the rain starts roaring down. I take this opportunity to focus the rain into my water skins, replenishing my entire pack. Hyo perks up and starts to stand, drinking her fill. I decide that I had better not stick around. If she is still hungry, I may well become her next meal.

I bow low to this magnificent creature. 'Goodbye and good luck, beautiful Hyo, may your adventures treat you well.'

No part of me wants to leave such a beautiful creature until I know it has full strength, but I feel this rain will bring back all of the necessities that will help her thrive once more. I wonder at this moment shared, and for a few minutes, I feel peaceful and happy that I have been blessed to share this moment with such a beautiful creature. A moment shared, a memory created, and perhaps a thread of sweet happiness before I get to the hell hole called Neodias.

I bow to the leopard once more, dashing off back towards my goal, the Metropolis.

Chapter 11 – The Slug

I wake to the sound of rain. Not a drop has touched me during my slumber. I never thought that I could control the elements in my sleep. If only Father were still here, perhaps he could have taught me more about these powers and how far they can be pushed. I didn't even get the chance to ask mother before I left. Should I have stayed and completed my training with her? I feel like I have barely extended my capabilities but have been left to stumble across their limitations, like a child lost in a dark forest. It's too late to worry about that now. I have a quest, and once it is over, I shall return to my mother, and she can become my master.

I collect my things and pack them into my bag. I don't have much to carry anymore, as finding food and water is easy in the forest I now dwell. Creatures roam free, berries and fruit are scattered everywhere, growing naturally with no human intervention. They seem to flourish here. Water flows from trees, pooling into the natural holes made by extending branches. I feel comfortable here. The weather is more changeable now, giving me the chance to practice and learn more for survival. I am still a student, but things are growing easier, my talents feel more natural, and I can use them with little thought.

If my parents were here, they would have relished this journey. We would have had the time to train hard, enjoy the scenery that has blown my mind, stalked creatures of all sorts, just to see how quiet we could be. They could have shown me everything I need to know. I feel lost, like being stranded in an ocean of fish, yet without the knowledge to net them. Why did he die? How could this have happened? The quiet calm of the forest does nothing to prevent my rage from surfacing. Each time I relive that moment, watching his body fall to the floor like a lifeless ragdoll, his kind face and mind scattered across the dirty ground.

The sound of heavy thunder awakens me from the daydream, well, less of a dream and more of a nightmare.

'I'm sorry, Father.'

I press on, listening to the rain falling on the canopy of branches above. The dull and constant patter of water striking the earth drowns out the noises of any close by creatures. Even sounds carried on the wind are weak and subdued. I must remain sharp. My eyes stay focused on the dark parts of the forest backdrop; I can't rely on the winds to inform me of roaming creatures or bandits in conditions like this.

I do wonder why we cannot control the water once it has struck the ground? I stop to experiment on a small pool of water. I watch as the larger drops of rainwater land in the pool, creating the tiniest of splashes. Can we control the splashes? I cross my legs and sit in a comfortable position, focusing my powers towards the puddle water, seeing if I can control the tiny drops that jump out of the water surface when another drop connects.

'Why can't I control you, damn it!' I shout at the water. 'I must be losing my mind, sat here, shouting at a puddle.'

I hear a quiet step behind me as swift as the wind as a large blunt object strikes the back of my head. I fall face first towards the sopping ground with a vicious ringing in my head. I try to stand, but another strike comes, sending me back to the ground as everything fades away into darkness.

I wake up soaking wet, covered in mud and with an unbearable headache. I glance around to see that I was dragged into a small opening. The forest's denseness gives way to a patch of open grass with a roof of branches from tall trees. The sound of a small crackling fire is close by, giving me some warmth and comfort in my otherwise cold and soggy state. It doesn't last long. I try to move but come to the realisation that my hands and feet are bound, tied tightly, making it impossible for me to free myself. The rope is thick and so rough that it gnaws into my skin.

'Ha, the poor soul is awake,' says an unfamiliar croaky voice.

'Well, ain't that a dandy, I thort I woulda killed him with that club to the head,' says another man.

As my consciousness returns to me, I am left face to face with two hideous looking men. They are both filthy, covered in mud, blood and whatever else that green gunk is that seems to be pouring from their wort ridden mouths. One of them smiles at me, revealing rotting, black teeth.

'Why don't the rain like ye?' The balding man with black eyes asks.

'Ain't you got no manners, Slug?' says the blue-eyed man, who has hair matted so densely, that I can't tell where the hair begins and the dirt ends. 'My name is Dug, and this right 'ere, is Slug.'

'May I ask why you have bound me, Dug?'

'Yes, you may ask,' he replies, a sinister grin on his face.

A few moments of silence pass, 'Well? Why am I bound?'

'I said you could ask. I didn't say I would tell you,' chuckles Dug proudly.

'You are a funny fecker, Dug,' adds Slug, tapping his friend on the shoulder. 'So, why don't the rain like you?'

I had gotten so used to being far from civilisation that I had forgotten to allow the rain to fall as usual when I am asleep. It seems to be the same if I have passed out or am unconscious too. I must remember that if I ever make it out of this situation.

'I don't understand what you mean?' I lie, sensing the men are not the sharpest blades in the armoury.

'What do you think of that, Slug? I think he is lying to us.'

'Yes, Dug, I do believe he be lying to us, alright.'

'Oh well, he may be a liar, but he looks healthy and delicious.'

Delicious…

Both men burst into laughter. Dug scurries off with an axe in tow and commences to chop down branches of nearby trees. Without the use of my hands, it makes it impossible to use my powers. My sword is at the other side of the opening, giving me no chance to crawl over without being seen.

'Help me,' I whisper, hoping the breeze can carry it to the ears of anyone that might be close. I hear the words drift off into the trees. Dug and Slug don't strike me as the most perceptive of fellows. Yet their skills in stealth and hunting must be second to none, but I'm sure they won't notice a slight whisper on the wind.

As the light starts to dim, Slug and Dug make the fire very hot. Burning wood is stacked up, the logs glow hot, as embers of orange and red dance around each other. It looks close to being ready for cooking. Its heat is now getting uncomfortable, causing sweat trails to run off my brow. The prospect of being eaten by a couple of cannibals may also be playing a part, mind you. I consider calling upon the rain to drop onto the fire, but the canopy of trees stops much from penetrating this tiny opening. My roof of branches and leaves makes me wish I was back in the protection of the weather, be it fierce or gentle.

'What shall we start with, Dug?'

'The legs, of course, Slug,' he looks at me, licking his lips with glee, and I shudder. 'Always the legs first. Once they are gone, he ain't gonna run far, is he.'

They both cackle with insane laughter, yet their eyes remain focused on me.

Slug moves over to a filthy sack laid by the fire, pulling from it a rusty saw.

'This e're, is *Toothy*,' he points, delicately pressing his fingertips to the serrated teeth upon his tool. 'She don't look like much, but those teeth will gnaw through your bones easy peasy,' he smiles, sculking over with a fierce hunger in his eyes.

I glance over to Dug, who is busy stoking the fire. He stares into it with a jackal-like grin underlining his crooked nose.

'Why are you doing this?' I ask, trying to delay Slug.

'Because we're hungry.'

'But the forest is bountiful? Food can be found everywhere if you know where to look.'

'Let me then ask ya this, Have you ever tried human before?'

'No, of course, I haven't.'

'Well then, let me tell ya; human meat is delicious. The young are tender and sweet, the old, tough and chewy and the fat, what about the fat, Dug?'

Dug gazes at his friend, eyes as wide as a full moon. 'My favourite, Slug. Chewing through the salty goodness of a fat thigh, dripping and succulent,' Dug lets out a hideous slurping sound as he pretends to lick and bite what I can only imagine being the leg of a past victim.

'You see?' Says Slug, 'We like them fat and juicy. It also helps that the fat ones can't run very far.'

'Can't you see what it's doing to you?' I plead.

'It makes us strong, Meat.'

'Meat?' I ask.

'Yes, Meat is your name, Meat. You see, my father was a butcher at Neodias. He always told me not to name the animals else they become pets, you see,' chuckles Slug.

'Nope, no pets,' adds Dug.

'Where is your father now?' I ask, praying there isn't another of them roaming this wood.

'Dead. He shouldn't have fed the boss men human. They didn't like it as we like it.'

The thought of it makes my stomach flip in waves of nausea. What chance did they have with a father like that?

'I…I'm sorry your father did this to you.'

Dug stops stoking the fire. He lollops over to the side of his equally insane brother. He holds a poker in his hand, the white-hot end of it smoulders, leaving a small trail of smoke behind. For the first time since my father died, I feel a fear boil within me. I managed to delay them temporarily, but it's too late. No one in this forest can help me now. My whispers probably lost to the trees, absorbed by the sounds of rustling leaves and the swaying of branches.

'You ain't be talking about me, father, Meat?' Dug's hungry gaze, turning into one of anger. He points the poker to my face.

'Stop playing with tha food, Dug.'

Dug lowers the poker, stabbing it into the ground by my side. It hisses as it cools on the damp floor, like a snake that missed its prey.

'Right we are then, time to cook,' says slug, still wielding *Toothy*.

I feel my heart speed up to a relentless cascade of thumps. Times up. 'Wait!'

'Erm, no. Your meat becomes our meat now, Meat.' Slug chuckles.

'You made a poem, Slug,' says Dug, tapping his brother on the back in congratulations.

What's that? Did I hear a new noise on the breeze? Not a voice, yet familiar. My concentration is torn away as I feel *Toothy* connect with my leg. The serrated teeth start being pulled and pushed over my flesh. It rips through it, the pain exquisite. All I can do is scream. My blood spits into the eyes of Slug, which seems to make his smile bigger and his eyes more focused. He licks the blood from his lips with delight. I feel everything start to go dark again as I almost pass out. Slug slaps me hard, drawing me back into the nightmare.

'The best bit is coming, no time to nap, Meat.'

I close my eyes, praying for the sun to heal me. I can feel it, just beyond the branches above. It reaches for me, and I for it. The patter of rain has subsided if only the roof of trees would part. *Toothy* reaches my thigh bone, showing me what pain is for the first time in my life. The intensity and fierceness of its bite make me wish for a swift death, not this slow torturous end. Blood is now leaking from my leg like a red river, and I wonder how my human frame can contain so much of it.

The grinding sensation halts. 'Dug, Come e're, help me with this. *Toothy* is stuck in the bone.'

In the moment of respite, I hear that familiar noise again. The wind urges me to stay awake, to fight this. I know that noise, yes! I remember now the sound of pad to ground.

The curtains of the forest wall suddenly burst open. With a mighty roar, Hyo, my feline friend, emerges, looking fierce and powerful. She leaps onto Dug, claws extended, ripping the cannibal's throat in a single swipe, leaving him gasping his final breath in a pool of his own blood. Slug shrieks with rage as he charges toward his club. Hyo, eyes Slug while he races towards the weapon, snarling at the crazed man. I throw myself to the floor, hoping that this distraction will keep Slug at bay till I can reach my sword. I drag myself across the muddy floor, each movement a reminder that *Toothy* remains within my thigh, it's metallic teeth constantly chewing into the bone and muscle of my leg. I glance to my left to see Slug and Hyo in a flurry of combat. I'm surprised by the agility of the man. He is truly an adept warrior despite his decrepit looks. He glides around Hyo with the grace of a weapon master. Hyo and he circle each other, the snarls from both man and beast are terrifying. I wait until Slug's back faces me and start to cut the ropes that bind my wrists on my blade. Hyo pounces at Slug, but he sidesteps swiftly and smashes his weapon into the head of the feline, who collapses in a concussed mess on the floor. I move fast, frantically slicing at the ropes and my wrists. I must stop Slug! The cannibal raises the club, letting out a furious roar, as he drives it downwards towards the neck of my friend. My wrists are freed, and with what little strength I have left, I summon the winds to wrap around my wrist, blasting it out towards the weapon heading towards Hyo. The power slams into the club, sending Slug's swing slightly off target and into the earth.

'You will pay for that, Meat!' he screams.

'I doubt that,' I respond, pointing to the now not so stunned Hyo, who, in a single swing, tears off the man's jaw. Slugs eyes widen for a moment as he realises his time is up. He slumps forward to his knees, attempting to say something to me, but all that I hear is a gargle of blood that pours from where his mouth and tongue used to be.

I feel my life force fading, the saw is still well wedged into my thigh, and I can now barely move. The breeze dances around me, trying to keep me awake, everything around me fading away, and I can feel my eyes closing, the darkness inviting me to feel the pain no more. With a great roar, Hyo shakes me from my drift, dragging my consciousness toward the light. I draw the wind back to my arm, giving as long as I can to allow a build-up of power. I point my fist towards the sky, releasing the force toward the canopy above. The wind energy blasts through the ceiling of branches above me, exposing a blue patch of heaven and a ball of life-giving heat and fire above. The small hole in the canopy of leaves allows a single ray of sunlight to cascade onto me. I absorb it instantly, feeling my body attempting to repair my flesh and rejuvenate my blood. I try to tug *toothy* out of my leg, but it is very stuck. I cry out in pain, hoping not to draw any creatures close and thus becoming easy prey.

'There's only one way this is coming out of my leg.' I grab my sword and hammer the saw blade several times with the hilt. I feel my bone snap as the saw falls to the ground, bloody and disgusting. I lie back, allowing the sun to work its magic as everything starts to go black. My last thoughts are of Hyo, how she saved me as I saved her, 'Thank you, friend.'

Part 2

Chapter 12 –Neodias, The Metropolis

A few days have passed since my run-in with Slug and Dug. My leg looks and feels like nothing had ever happened, thanks to my friend, the Sun. The forest is thinning; the trees that usually shroud every corner of my world are growing smaller and fewer. The sun finds it easier to push itself through the branches, and the animals that dwell within the deeper parts of the wood, are nowhere to be seen. Hyo had left too, without waiting for me to wake. She knew I would be okay and went back to her home, no doubt. I can't explain why a creature such as she could have such a strong connection with me. We saved each other, and I only wish I could have thanked her somehow. I will never forget you, Hyo, my feline friend.

The seasons seem to be changing. The green I had grown accustomed to is replaced with golden browns and sunkissed oranges. The leaves are starting to abandon their grasp of the branches that hold them. Even the gentle caress of the wind seems enough to prise them from their resting place. Some fall directly to the ground while others gracefully imitate the winds dance, swaying left to right and swirling around an invisible playground. It is a wonder to watch. They create a beautiful patchwork blanket on the forest floor, a multitude of autumnal colours giving the notions of an ocean being admired as the sun sets on its horizon. It is quite strange that I can feel so peaceful here, considering the chaos that ensued just a few days ago deeper within the belly of the forest. I take a deep breath, absorbing it all in one last time before I step out beyond the wall of bark and branches into an opening.

My eyes are instantaneously drawn to the massive darkness amongst the greens, browns and oranges. The flats beyond the clearing look like they have a cancerous growth exuding from its side. A high wall surrounds buildings as tall as the heavens, reaching up as if grasping at the sky with black/grey claws. I have never seen anything like this before. On the outskirts of the wall, there are various groupings of smaller homes, or I think that's what they are?

I quicken my pace now, excited to see what exists within the gargantuan buildings. Maybe the gods themselves live atop them? Perhaps kings? Kings from lands that I have never seen, full of knowledge and wonder. Hopefully, they can tell me of this man, the Archivist that destroyed my family and sent me on this journey. I guess I will know the answer soon enough. It must be a very safe place, with walls this size. The expelling of folks like Slug and Dug means they have morals and undoubtedly a vast array of well-trained soldiers who keep the peace. At least I will not have to care about the fury of the wilderness anymore. I think I will like this place despite its hellish look.

My excitement gets the better of me, and I break into a run, absorbing just enough sun to keep me from tiring, yet not too much that I run too fast. I must not make a scene when I arrive, or else they will never allow me inside. As the city gets closer, the sheer size of it becomes even more apparent. It dawns on me that I must find one man within those great walls. Where will I begin? Perhaps it is a close-knit community, and they will all know each other? I try not to allow myself to get overwhelmed at the task I have set before me by focusing on getting there in one piece. If I have to ask every single person I meet, I will. Yet, I'm curious about my reaction to this evil man once I meet him. I have never had to face such an opponent, and my father always warned me to stay calm in the face of adversity. Will I manage that? I hope so. I would hate to disappoint the man that made me who I am today.

As I approach the hive of buildings, I notice that the houses situated outside the walls have been built from nought but scraps. The hovels begin as a minor littering of homes, yet as I approach the main gates, the surrounding buildings become far denser. Some of them are built on the top of another, all placed together like a broken jigsaw, the pieces forced together to make an abstract image. The people living within them look at me wearily, their faces covered with grime. Their grey, torn clothing seems as though it were passed from generation to generation or sewn together from clothing scraps. I did not expect such things from a place so grand. Surely within the city is an endless amount of resources? I also passed many rivers en route. Why do they not go there with buckets and fishing rods?

The water can provide much sustenance, and they would be clean. The fish I caught and gorged on threw themselves on my fire; they were so plentiful?

I approach one of the families 'Excuse me, friends. What is this place?' I ask.

The family rushes back into their ramshackle home, completely ignoring my question, seemingly frightened of me. I keep walking, attempting to make eye contact with a few more families, which yields the same reaction each time. If I don't approach them, they gaze at me with a hunger in their eyes. I feel for these people; no one should live like this, yet I cannot help but wonder why they don't help themselves? The wall must be two hundred feet tall, and from what I can see, it covers the entire city circumference. The entrance has a massive metal door, large enough for both man and beast of any size. Contained within it is another smaller door, probably there to allow individuals through so as not to waste time having to prise open these heavy entryways. The smaller entrance is guarded by six large soldiers, clad in a steel breastplate and wielding halberds and short swords. They look sturdy, and their attire is well kept and pristine, especially if you compare them to the typical resident out here.

'Hello,' I say as I advance towards them. 'I would like entry to Neodias, please.'

'What business do you have in the city, boy?'

'I seek a man.'

'A man ey,' the guards chuckle to each other, 'there are plenty of men in here, one to suit every taste, even that of a farm boy.'

I feel he is attempting to insult me, yet I don't understand. 'I am searching for someone.'

'Well, that narrows it down. What is this mans name?'

'I don't know?'

'OK, what does he look like?'

'I… I don't know that either.'

'Oh well, not to worry, come on in.'

'Really!'

'No. Get out of here and back to your farm, boy. You have no business here.' All the guards start laughing.

This place is hideous. I understand they have to guard the entrance but have they no manners?

Have they not studied Bushido to become warriors? They know nothing of honour and integrity. I wish I could teach them a lesson, but that would be a terrible idea in front of all these people. They are scared enough. Plus, it would draw unwanted attention in a time where I must tread carefully.

I wait for the sun to sleep and the stars to wake and start walking around the city's wall. It is lit with nought but a few torches. The fires created by those living within the shacks cast shadows of humans and buildings alike upon the great wall. I can take advantage of this terrible light. People surround the small fires in tiny communities, all trying the cosy up for warmth and light. For me, the good part of that is that gazing into the fire will ruin their night vision, making it easier for me to blend into the shadows unnoticed. I skulk around the outskirts, looking for an ideal and quiet spot to make my move. I cannot be noticed, or the game will be over before it has even begun.

I find a perfect spot with very few houses, even less light. The people that reside here are quiet and sit there watching the flames dance, that same look of hunger as if they imagine some fresh meat or fish cooking upon it. Just as predicted, the guards are on patrol. They strut by, unaware of my presence in the shadows. They take little notice of the dwellers here, talking and laughing amongst themselves, hands-on swords, but loosely. If anyone were to attack, they would not be ready. As they leave the area, I start to clamber up the buildings. I am amazed to find that some of the shacks are built onto the actual wall and that some of them have been haphazardly assembled on top of each other. This building is three stories high, with small metallic ramps making it possible to reach these so-called homes' front doors. I would not like to test the stability of these ramshackle pathways, and so I don't. I allow the winds to swirl around my ankles, lifting me an inch off the ground, making me lightfooted and silent. Occasionally, I give myself a boost, leaping on to the next roof until I am at the top of the third tier.

This last section of the wall is still very high. To reach the summit, I will have to get a little help. A distraction will ensure I am not seen. Something small that won't cause any harm. I know what will work. I start to gather the wind around me while hidden in the dark corners of the roof. Being careful not to be seen, I stand up and away from my position and fire separate bursts of wind at all the torches in the area. One by one, I extinguish them, causing the guards and locals to panic. They draw swords and fall into a close combat formation, the four of them creating a box by standing back to back as if surrounded by an unknown enemy. I am impressed at how quickly they react. I will not underestimate them if we ever end up in combat, and I notice that despite their lack of manners, they are well trained. The last torch goes out and throws the entire area into darkness, and that is my cue to make a move. Gathering the wind again, I coil it around my ankles and leap, the force of it firing me into the black sky above. I see the top of the wall, and, using small bursts from my wrist, I fall gracefully towards the top. I land softly and silently, just as my father taught me. I see guards patrolling the roof, this time armed with bows and short swords. I make for the shadows again and wait for them to pass.

I jump from darkness until I am gazing over the opposite edge of the great wall. Never have I seen such splendour in one place. The enormous grey buildings reach higher than the wall itself. They are what I imagine a giants gravestone to resemble. Perhaps the tombstone of the story of Goliath. My mother loved telling me that story. Even the modest can make a difference against all odds if you have the fight in you to do so. The small buildings are enormous in comparison to the farms back home. Below them, on the ground level, there is so much light that the towers cast a shadow over the city's smaller stretches. I wonder if the people who live amongst these smaller areas ever see sunlight? The citizens are rushing around, even at this late hour, like locusts through a cornfield. I can imagine them devouring all in their path. They seem nothing like the husks of humans that remain outside the complex. They are all moving with purpose, yet what purpose? I am excited to find out. A feeling of desperation hits me. How will I find the Archivist amongst all this? There must be hundreds of thousands of people. How am I to find one man?

I look for a quiet landing point amongst the chaos below. The inside is considerably cleaner than the out, and buildings are not attached to the wall like the outer perimeter's shacks. I make my way along the wall weaving in and out of the darkness that the torchlight cannot touch. The only problem is that I will have to find a dark spot to leap into, and then I will be landing on the unknown. Hopefully, my night vision will return in time for me to see where I'm going. I spot a potential; for some reason, no one seems to be moving in that area, the darkness would make it impossible for anyone to see my landing and no torches light this part of the city. I swirl the wind around my ankles, leaping into the darkness, praying my faith in this shrouded place is not misplaced. My faith, however, was wrong. As I approach the bottom of the wall, the smell of whatever is in the darkness starts to make itself apparent. I land with a splash and the stench of what can only be putrid human faeces. My eyes water with the horrific smells I have fallen upon. I trample out of the muck and grime and onto the ledge of the cesspit, shaking off my clothing as best I can and make my way into the light. At least I was correct in my judgement of it having no people here. Unfortunately, I can now see and smell why.

The people here are very different from anything I have seen before. They wear jackets and trousers that are patterned, vibrant and made of cotton. This clothing offers zero protection from the elements and even less protection in combat. They are fancy, and the people here resemble peacocks, all adorning bright colours and large hats of sorts. Feathers cover dresses that the women can barely walk in, yet all are rushing around like time is an expense. The occasional nod between people is all I see in the way of communication or a slight tip of a hat to a fellow wearing the same colours. The women walk with straight backs, gliding strides and a slit up their skirts to show off their legs and god knows what else. I make my way into the bustling crowds; It is so light here that it could be midday. It hugely contrasts the lives outside the wall. The poor, rotting people and homes on the other side of this fortress living a constant struggle for survival, yet this place is vibrant and luxurious. The people look healthy and some even fat. However, I do wonder how they can get so when they rush around like worker ants. How do they manage to eat so much when there are people who are starving on the outside? It makes no sense.

I stop for a moment, taking in the environment. The menacingly large grey structures reach up so high that I feel you could see above the clouds on a rainy day. I wonder if the sun is always visible up there? I could have a constant source of power from the top. Apart from these massive stone buildings, the smell of the place is distinct. Even through the stench of my clothing, the beautiful scents of food and flowers are everywhere. I imagine an orchid plantation would smell like this. Sometimes I get wafts of citrus fruits, zesty oranges and lemons, then the beautiful calming scents of lavender or chamomile, yet twinned with that of roasting vegetables and meats in a coat of spices that makes my stomach grumble. I have not eaten a proper meal since I left home some weeks ago. I decided to follow my nose and find some food. Drifting through the crowds is hard work. They all seem to walk like salmon swim. You either walk with them or fight against them. I guess that is similar to how my father taught me the wind works. I go with the flow, following precious smells and swanky clothing till I stumble into a marketplace. My eyes widen at the plethora of foods laid out within the stalls. People are shouting out into the crowds about what the food contains with almost poetic descriptions of the various offerings making my stomach grumble once more.

A woman points at me. 'Ello dear, why don't you try one of Holly's dumplins.'

'Oh hello, don't you mind if I do? These look delicious.'

My mouth is already watering at the prospect of chewing into one of these delicious balls of meat. I take a bite, and instantly the memories of my mothers cooking come flooding back—perfectly cooked meat, wrapped in pastry which is coated in salt and pepper. The flavours make my taste buds weep tears of joy., I devour the morsel in no time at all.

'You're a hungry one,' she says to me, handing over a tray of delights.

'These are amazing. Thank you so much. I haven't eaten anything like this in weeks.'

'That's okay, lad. I'm glad you have enjoyed them. If only all my customers had appetites like yours, I could close early every day,' she chuckles. 'Now, these are five coppers each,' she smiles, opening her hand out to me.

'Excuse me?'

'You must pay, boy,' her smile quickly drops to a frown, her kind, grandmother like face suddenly turns to that of a woman scorned, and my mother always used to say, a woman scorned is not to be trifled with.

'I have no money. I have travelled very far. Perhaps I can offer an alternative? Maybe you need some things lifted or shifted? I am strong; I can help.'

'What I want, farm boy, is the coin. You thought I was doing this through charity? Now pay else I call the guards!'

'Please do not do that. I can get you the coin. Can you give me a few days?'

'No... GUARDS!' She starts shouting at the top of her voice, much louder than I expect from an old lady. 'Guards, thief. THIEF!'

Her hollering starts to draw a crowd. Most of them look at me in disgust. I'm not sure if it is because I'm being called a thief or because my clothes are covered in muck? I start to run, zipping in and out of the crowds. A couple of guards begin to give chase, the regular folks pointing in my direction to give me away. I do not blame them, I have stolen, and I wouldn't be happy with that either. The guards, however, are slow. Their steel breastplate makes it difficult for them to keep up, and that matched with a sizable halberd, they don't stand a chance. I weave in and out of the crowds expertly, and in a few moments, I lose them. I slow my pace, attempting to blend in. Not an easy task when you are wearing leather armour and filthy clothes, and everyone else is in fancy suits of bright reds, yellows and blues. My smell is probably not helping my cause much either.

I duck into an alleyway to gather my thoughts, catching my breath a little to decide what my next plan of action shall be. I have heard of this coin for payment, but our village worked by everyone contributing to society and helping where it was in need, or even by simple trade. It wouldn't be rare for my father to send me with mothers food to the older folk, making sure they were well fed and not cold. Only now do I realise what a caring community my parents built. I miss it.

The alley is not the most pleasant place to rest, but it is quiet, which is a rarity here. I sit down and take a deep breath to gather my thoughts.

'This archivist must be known by people. No one could have murdered my father with such a weapon unless he is already known, if not famous.'

I close my eyes for a moment. I hadn't realised how tiring the journey had been. And with the sun going down, I cannot absorb its power to replenish my energy. I still need to sleep. Your brain always needs a reset, my mother used to say. I could do with her wisdom right now and her positivity. It broke me to see her so crushed. I only hope I can find the man responsible and ask him why he killed my father. I must reclaim Senso and get revenge for my family.

Chapter 13 – The Man in the White Suit

I have been in the city for a few days now, getting my bearings and trying to find out as much as I can about the Archivist. Unfortunately, this has got me nowhere. I have been asking everyone I can, yet no one wishes to speak to me. Each time I try, they look at me, seeing that I don't belong, shout for the guards, or simply walk away. Either way, I need to change my plan. There are hundreds of thousands of people here. How will I ask them all? It would take me years.

Today, as I get up and stretch from another night of sleeping in my favoured alleyway, the bustle of the crowd is more frantic then I have ever seen before. People are not just rushing but running towards something. I follow as swiftly as possible, taking in the excitement that everyone else seems to be feeling. As we all approach a large open square, I see a man stood on a vast wooden stage. He stands still, waiting for something, I have no idea what, but his poise tells me it will be something epic. He raises his fists into the air.

'Yes! Yes, people, it is that time again,' the man in the white suit shouts.

The crowd go crazy, screaming back at the man in joy, waving their arms and flailing in a frenzy.

'That's right, the gladiators have been training hard, and tonight, the battles begin. You have been patient, and you shall be rewarded.' He points to the crowd.

I ask the man next to me, 'What's going on here?'

'Where have you been? Living in a cave?'

'No, well actually, a few nights ago I had to find shelter in a cave? What does that have to do with this?'

'Nothing…'

Before I get the chance to ask any more questions, he moves away, shaking his head in the process. I fixate my eyes on the man in the white suit.

'Gladitorial betting will commence soon. Who will your coin be on?' The Viking? The Barbarian? Or perhaps one of the new contenders? Either way, this is your chance to make it big and into the centre of Neodias. Where only the rich reside!'

The crowds cheer and chant again, calling out at the man in white in a frenzy. Gladiatorial combat, I have not heard of this before? Combat has never been a sport but a means of survival. I must know more. If the man that can kill my father from a mile away knows of this contest, perhaps he will enter? I can't imagine many that could best a man such as he. I push my way through the people, trying to get closer to the man in white. Perhaps I can ask him if the Archivist is entering the contest. After a few minutes of pushing and getting stamped on by bystanders, I make it to the front. I ignore peoples disdain at my shoving, this is far more important, and the Archivist must be stopped.

'Excuse me, man in white? Excuse me?' He can't hear me. The crowds are too loud. I must try something else. With a small calling of the breeze, I leap onto the platform and approach the white-suited man. As swiftly as I land on the stage to ask my question, two guards are upon me.

'Wait, please, I just need to ask this man a question.' I had forgotten that my weapon is attached to my back, making it seem as though I intend to do the man in white harm.

Before I have the chance to explain myself, swords are drawn. They charge at me, and I hear the crowd's excitement rise. The first guard takes a swing at me, but with my sun-enhanced speed, I dodge it easily. The other thrust his sword forward. I catch the blade in my hand and swiftly kick him in the hand, making him release the weapon. I trip his ankles with a circular sweep of my leg, and he plummets to the ground and into the crowd below. The second soldier takes another swing at me. I parry his sword with the hilt of the weapon in my grasp. I spin behind my attacker connecting the sword's handle into the back of the man's knee, and he drops forward.

'I do not wish to fight you.'

'Then what is it you want, boy?' Asks the man in white.

'Is a man called the Archivist fighting in your tournament?'

The man in white pauses for a moment. He seems unphased by the combat between us.

'Yes, yes he is.'

'I must meet him. He owes me a great debt. He is an evil man!'

'First, you must meet these.' He points to another group of soldiers who are making their way towards the platform. 'Now, if you can beat six elite soldiers, I will be impressed.'

I don't stick around to find out what is so special about these soldiers, and I leap off the side of the platform, collecting a fraction of wind at my feet. I bounce off the heads of some of the onlookers and drop into the dense group of people. Staying low, I slink between them, careful not to be seen by these elite guards. I can hear the man in the white suit start chanting again, the people joining him in a flailing of their arms. They take very little notice of me as I escape out into the open, pausing to look back at the man in white. He looks directly at me, a wry smile spreading across his face. I rush away and back to my alleyway. The man I seek *is* in the tournament after all. Now to find out where it is and how I can get in.

Despite my attempts at staying anonymous, my latest adventure out into the city makes me realise that I made quite an impact during my idiotic stunt with the man in white. Wanted posters are now starting to appear with my face on, disturbing the peace and attacking a soldier of the law. All I wanted to do was ask a question. They attacked me, and I merely defended myself. How can I explain this to them? Perhaps they will understand if I tell them of the murder of my father? Yet, from what I have seen so far, these soldiers are not to be reasoned with or in the mood for chit chat. How do I stay anonymous long enough for them to forget me, and how do I get to fight in this gladiatorial competition?

I venture back to my alley, needing time to think and to plan. If I decide to sign up, that will mean showing my face, which will instantly get me arrested. I arrive at my make-shift home and plonk myself on the ground, sitting cross-legged to meditate and hopefully come up with some answers. My stomach is making its usual gurgling noises, but I have got more used to the feeling of hunger. Thankfully, as long as the sun is out, I can use its power to regenerate my energy levels, I will remain hungry, but I will not be weak.

The light starts to drift away, and the glowing orange sun drops out of sight and beyond the huge buildings that cast a shadow over my alley. The sun still gives me a feeling of warmth, and I cannot help but be mesmerised by it's falling. I think it is my favourite time of day. The sky looks like a fire from the heavens has lighted it. The orange and red glow of red hot coals or wood. I miss the smell of real fire, life-giving and warming on a winters day. I wonder what it is like up there with the angels? Do they watch us? Do they crave to be here with us? If my father were still here, he would have the answers; of this, I am certain.

It gets darker, and the sky turns from pink to purple before giving itself up to the night and stars of the night. I store the suns energy within me to help me stay warm on the colder evenings. I did not plan for this well and brought no blankets or extra clothing with me, just what I am wearing and my leather armour. I start to drift into a deep meditation, contemplating my next move and how I can not only survive here but keep up the search for the man that ruined my family.

I am startled out of my dream by the sound of heavy footsteps. A small group of people are walking down my alley. I stay completely still, barely breathing and wait. Perhaps they will miss me lying here in the mud, rubbish and shadows. The familiar face of the man in white pushes past the group and searches around the alley. I have nowhere to run and nowhere else to hide, damn myself for choosing a place with no escape routes. It takes him mere minutes of searching for his gaze to meet my own. That same wry smile appearing on his face.

'You, boy, I am glad I found you,' he says, spotting me huddled up.

'I am sorry about the soldiers. It was not my intention to hurt them. I just wanted to ask you a question.'

'Please, do not worry about those. They are my guards, and I have explained that they are to remove the posters and to leave you be.'

'Thank you, but why?'

'You are a talented boy, and I want you to listen to a proposition I have. First of all, let's get you in some proper clothes, feed you and allow you to wash. I look after my people, and I intend to convince you to enter my employment. What do you say?' He holds out a hand to me.

He seems like a nice man; I grab his hand and allow him to help me up. The men around him look like warriors but very well kept warriors. They have no armour, but their weapons shine like they are brand new. The fierce and controlled look in their eyes makes me believe that they are outstanding fighters and very well paid soldiers by the rest of their attire. Their clothing is subdued and subtle. Shades of grey cotton, loosely fitted to not obstruct their movements should they need to fight. They show no fear, and although they seem ready to spring into action in a breath, they do not seem tense.

'Come, friend, let's get you sorted out and then we can talk. What shall I call you?'

'My name is Jacob, sir.'

'Ok, Jacob, it is a pleasure to meet you, and please, call me Ajax.'

We leave the alley, and waiting for us is a grand carriage which looks to be made of dark mahogany wood, varnished heavily with symbols of a crossed sword and axe coated in gold leaf. Four beautiful white horses are pulling the carriage. The contrast between the carriage and the beasts is unreal, making them look ethereal. I have never seen such clean horses. They almost seem to shine like polished platinum even in this darkness and smog.

'They are called Akhal-Teke horses. Are they not the most beautiful creatures you have ever seen?'

'Yes, they truly are a wonder to set eyes upon, Ajax. I once met a single creature more beautiful though, her name was Hyo, and she was magnificent,' I respond.

'I would like to meet this...?'

'She was a leopard, and I wish I could introduce you, but alas, she is wild and in the forest where she belongs.'

'That is a shame. Sometimes, a beast needs to be wild and live free and other times, a beast needs to be captured to help man. Obviously, man then needs to ensure they treat the creature with respect, protect it and look after it,' I feel him looking at me for a response, but I keep my gaze forward and step into the carriage.

The interior is grander than the outside, the seats are a plush, soft leather, and the dark wood finish has been carved into the shapes of the horses that pull this very cart. The horses are encrusted in gems and more gold leaf, making them shine like the ones outside. Even the smell inside here is beautiful. The gentle scent of flowers and fresh grass reminds me of the meadows of my home. I long to close my eyes and be transported back there. How has he created such splendour?

'Magical, isn't it?'

'Like nothing I have ever experienced before,' I reply.

'I had this carriage commissioned by one of the most talented wood crafters in the entire city, the gems are from all over the world, and the gold leaf has been salvaged from melted down artefacts of the past. I have spent a lot of money to make it look like this.'

I touch the inside of the carriage, feeling the craftsmanship, taking it all in while inhaling the beautiful smells. This is something else - this is something spectacular.

'The smells, well that is created by oils, look,' he opens up a small compartment in the wall and dips his finger in a liquid within it. I inhale deeply, and my senses explode with glee.

'I can see you are impressed. Well, I can offer you all of this and more. I will explain more, but for now, let's get you washed and fed as I promised.'

Ajax knocks on the roof, and I hear the crack of a whip as the carriage begins to roll.

Chapter 14 – A Warriors Feast

The carriage halts, and the door is opened by a very well dressed man. He wears all black and a funny-looking hat which has a single white feather in it.

'Hello Master Ajax, welcome home,' he says with a bow.

'Thank you, Archie. Please prepare a bath for Jacob. He will be staying. Also, please can you make sure that food and one of the madames elixirs are prepared as soon as possible. This poor young fellow is so hungry I used his grumbling stomach to find him in the alley.' They both chuckle to each other, and Archie bows to Ajax.

'The food is already being prepared, Master, as is a room. I shall, with your permission, clean and stable the horses.'

'Thank you once again, Archie. I have no idea what I would do without you.'

Archie bows once again and strolls over to the horses. Ajax gestures for me to follow, and we walk towards a humble sized house. I was expecting a man of this stature to be living in one of the buildings that scrape the heavens. The house is still beautiful, and the gardens it is situated in are lush, green and exotic.

'Welcome to my humble home, Jacob.'

'Why don't you live in one of those heaven scrapers?'

'I choose not to. I find them a little overpowering and crude, wouldn't you agree? You couldn't have a garden such as mine in a place like that.'

'That is very true, and please don't be offended. Your home is beautiful.'

'Come inside and have a look for yourself, Jacob. I don't think you will be disappointed.'

Ajax opens the door using a small device that seems to unlock it. Inside, the home is stunning. Floors covered in furs and walls with lifelike paintings of people and places adorn them. A grand fireplace is in the centre of the room, the flames themselves reaching high yet not burning the ceiling, that is at least double the height of my own home. The room is warm, inviting and full of colour. I'm sure that all of these paintings tell a story.

'Wow! This is even more beautiful on the inside. Did you paint these pictures?'

'Sir, please remove your shoes.' Says another man dressed in black.

'Oh, so sorry, I bow to him and remove my shoes at the door.'

'Would you like me to burn them, Master Ajax?'

'Yes please, but you may as well wait. His clothing will be experiencing the same fate.'

'You can't burn my stuff. I need them,' I protest.

'Jacob, I will be providing you with less… uninviting clothing. You currently look like the homeless on the outside of the wall. We can't have that.'

'Oh, ok. You are far too kind, but my mother made me these.'

'The sword, please, sir,' the man dressed in black asks again.

'My sword. That is the one thing I cannot give up. No other finery could or will ever replace this blade. It was given to me by my father, and it doesn't leave my side.

'Do not worry, Jacob. We will not destroy the sword. It just isn't the best dinner attire,' Ajax smiles softly.

'Okay, but please may I just leave it here. I'd rather still have it within my reach.'

'I have no idea what you expect to happen here, Jacob, but I can assure you that you are safer here than anywhere else in the city. I have no quarrel with you leaving it by the door if it serves to ease your mind.' Ajax bows to me, gesturing toward the door.

I remove the weapon from my back and place it down.

'Thank you for understanding.'

'It is my pleasure. Now please, follow Archie. He will take you to one of the bathing suites and ensure you are clean for dinner.'

I nod in agreement and follow this new Archie. I wonder why he calls all of them by the same name?

I am taken to another beautiful room. A bath steams in the centre, and the smells are once again out of this world. This time lavender is the most potent scent that I can make out. Its soothing aromas remind me of what my mother placed on my pillow as a babe to help me sleep and calm my spirit. It suddenly makes sense when I walk up the edge and see the herb floating about in the hot, steaming water. The bath can easily hold five or six people in it. It seems like such a waste of water to have all this for just me.

'Please remove your clothes, Sir.'

'Call me Jacob, Archie. No need for all this Sir stuff.'

'As you wish, Jacob.'

'What is it like to work for such a man? Did you get all this finery when Ajax employed you?'

'I feel our positions are slightly different, Jacob. It is within his interest to win you over. For me, it was a matter of being good at my job and needing money.'

'Oh, I see, so I guess he doesn't want me to do what you do then?'

'You will see what he wants from you in due course, I am sure.'

I remove my clothes and step into the huge bath. I instantly feel my body start to relax. The dirt and grime seep off my body, but somehow the water remains clean.

'Archie, why is my water staying clean? I don't understand this magic?'

'It is a simple filtration system. The water is constantly flowing through the tub. My master doesn't like any dirt on him, so he created this. He believes that this way can you be truly clean when you bathe.'

'That's pretty clever. What an impressive man.'

'Yes, isn't he just.'

Once I am free from the dirt and grime, I stand in front of the mirror and barely recognise myself. I look skinny yet strong and lean. My journey so far has put me through a lot, but I feel better for it. Archie arrives with some new clothing for me, trousers of sorts and a top which goes over my head and has full sleeves. Its material is so soft. It gently caresses my skin as I put it on, making the hair on my body stand. These are the most comfortable clothes I have ever worn, although they seem flimsy and light. I doubt they would last long in the wilderness or even a light sparring session, but I will enjoy their comfort for now.

Archie leads me into another room. This one as grand as the others. In the middle is a large table full of food. My stomach instantly starts grumbling, and I remember how hungry I am. I see Ajax sitting, waiting for my arrival. He tucks a piece of material onto his shirt and waves me over.

'Have a seat, Jacob.'

'This food looks incredible.'

'You can eat as much as you can stomach, so please, have your fill.'

'Thank you so much. No one, besides my parents, has ever been this kind to me. I owe you.'

'Oh, please do not fret. You will have time to pay me back. I am sure.'

I tear my way through the feast before us, forgetting my place and my manners, it would seem, yet Ajax smiles. I realise that the material he placed on his shirt is to protect it from sauces and suchlike. He really does hate getting dirty. I eat myself into a stupor, filling my belly like it will not get a meal again for weeks, which, who knows, could be factual.

'Please grab the elixir, would you, Archie.'

'Of course, Master, very good.'

Off Archie trots to grab whatever this elixir is. He stands and walks so prim and proper, a practised way of moving with such elegance. The people here are so different from the little village I live in. I wonder how my mother is and what she would think of such gluttony? She would probably be giving me hell right now, seeing as I ate enough to feed four people.

'How are you feeling, Jacob?' Asks Ajax.

'I feel great. You know how to look after your guests.'

'Then why the concern on your face?'

'I was thinking of home and my mother, what she would think of all this.'

'What do you think she would say?'

'That I will get fat if I don't stop eating,' I chuckle while shovelling more food into my face.

Ajax laughs along with me. 'She sounds like a funny lady.'

'She's amazing, a true warrior and a perfect mother. It makes me sad to think of her alone back at the village.'

'Why is she alone?'

'My father was murdered, struck by a weapon from a mile away with no reason or warning. Part of her died that day. Part of us all did.'

'I... I am sorry to hear that, Jacob. It must have been a very difficult time for you.'

'It was, but if it weren't for that, I wouldn't be here searching for the man I asked about.'

'This Archivist you spoke of while I was talking to the rabble?'

'Rabble? What is a rabble?'

'The people, the people of this city. I call them a rabble because they run around like headless chickens, working and fucking and working and eating. No real purpose and no real drive.'

'Okay, so they are referred to as rabble. I will remember that.'

Archie returns with two glasses of liquid. He places one before me and takes the other to Ajax. It smells of blueberries and mint and looks delicious.

'To your health and prowess, Jacob.'

'To your health too, Ajax, and thank you for spoiling me like this.'

We bang our glasses together and down our beverages in one.

'Jacob, do you know what I do?'

'Nope, no idea at all.'

'I am an owner of prize beasts, much like the horses you saw today. Although I don't always deal with that sort of beast.'

'I don't understand?'

'I deal in warriors. My job is to create and provide the best and most entertaining gladiators in the lower tier stages of combat battlegrounds. You see, my father used to keep slaves. He taught me how to spot the strong from the weak, and Jacob; you are exceptional.'

'I still don't understand.'

'You are going to fight for me, and when you win, you and I will both make a lot of money.'

'I am not here to fight. I am here to find my fathers murderer.'

'I am afraid that you don't have much choice.'

'I always have a choice.'

'You are a wanted man, and I have spent this time and money to show you what you can have. People have killed for less, and all those poor souls outside the walls would sell their families for the chance I am giving you. Don't put up a fight, Jacob.'

'I don't like this. I want to leave.' I try to stand up, but my legs do not comply. I am paralysed. 'What have you done?'

'I have given you my special elixir, it renders you unconscious after a few minutes of drinking, and I must say, I am already impressed with your resilience toward it. Most men have passed out almost instantly, but here you are, still chatting away to me.'

'I will not fight for you!'

'You have no choice. If you don't fight, you will die. Jacob, you don't understand yet, but you will soon, and you will love it, I promise. You have what it takes to make both of us far more famous then I could have ever imagined. You are going to be a god amongst men, and I will ensure the world knows it.'

I feel my vision blur.

'Archie, take him to the cages and get him ready. He fights tomorrow.'

'Tomorrow, isn't that too soon?'

'No, I have a feeling that this one needs no training, so let's throw him in the deep and see what happens.'

'As you wish, Master.'

Chapter 15 – Death

'Wake, friend. It is your time. Wake, or you will be whipped.'

All I can muster is a groan, the groggy feeling still fogging my brain.

'You are about to enter the third tier arena, don't die here. You must stand and fight,'

I try to focus; my senses struggle to grasp or make sense of my environment. As my vision starts returning, I see a huge man standing beside me, shaking me gently. He is bleeding from above his eyebrow but seems none the worse for it. His dark skin covered in some sort of oil would make his almost naked body shine like that of a god if that god decided to roll in the mud and get stabbed in the head.

'What is this place?' I ask him.

'This is the tier three battleground, friend. You have been unconscious all day, but it is your time soon. The current battle is almost over, and you will fight next.'

'Fight? I don't wish to fight, why, and who am I fighting?' It floods back to me. Ajax, that bastard captured me.

'You are to fight Resin, the poison master. He will cut you in places and make you bleed out. That is how he toys with his prey. I do hope you win, though friend, else I will be fighting him next time,' the unusual man says, smiling broadly.

It is a strange sight, seeing this man, covered in mud and blood, cheerfully conversing with me before a battle. I manage to stand, but my legs still feel weak. I pray that the day is a sunny one. I hear the gurgling scream of a man and the cheering of a crowd. This is no battleground. It is a showground.

'I will not fight,' I say to the man.

'You think you won't fight? We all tried not to fight, but let me save you the trouble by telling you that there are two choices here. You fight and don't die, or you fight, and you do die.'

'I will escape. I will refuse to fight and reason with the other warrior.'

'You will reason with Resin?' The man laughs heartily, clutching his stomach. 'There is no reasoning with him. You will fight, and you will kill him, or you will be gone and thrown into the pit to rot with the rest of the losers. It has not been your day so far, friend, but maybe you can change that,' the man's smile turns serious.

A guard approaches and takes hold of my chains, pulling me forward towards the large iron doorways ahead. Small beams of light are sneaking into the otherwise dark room we are being held in. As my senses start to return, all I can smell is blood, death and faeces. Where am I?

The doors swing open, and another four guards greet me, all dressed in the attire I had seen on the soldiers of Ajax on our first meeting in the square. My eyes, sensitive to the light, start to make out shapes within the grounds' searing brightness. I instinctively try to absorb the sun, yet nothing is happening. The dark shapes begin to take familiar forms. I see a body being dragged away, the blood from the man spewing out in a trail behind his now lifeless corpse. His left arm dangles by threads of muscle, and his throat looks to have been gnawed off.

The floor is relatively small, enough for maybe twenty men. Above the ground level are stands that run circular to the arena. They are full of filthy looking people, somewhat similar to those I had met outside the gates of the great wall. They gaze at me like a butcher about to slaughter a fat pig. A frenzied expectancy for death and gore appears to have placed them in some sort of frantic trance, eyes as wide as saucers with glee.

'We have a new body for the arena today, folks!' A voice booms into the crowd. 'Handpicked by yours truly,' I recognise that voice, Ajax.

The crowd screams at him with hysteria. 'Yes, good people. Will this newcomer be able to beat the fury of Resin?'

The whole arena hoots with sounds of disgust and laughter, the crowd spitting in my direction.

'Come now; we are yet to have a surprising victory today. Resin could find himself in tier two should he win and against a newcomer. I think I know who I would bet on.'

The crowd once again flail and cheer like wild people. I see a slender looking man walk through the double gates opposite my own. His body is taut and scarred. He reminds me of Dug and Slug. I can't tell his age. His face has too many marks and is covered in tattoos that look to have been warn by blades and blunt objects over time. The amount of damage I can see, even from this distance, makes me wonder how this man has survived the trials he has been through. He sneers at me, dark eyes fixed on his target, rage burning within.

'Let the battlegrounds taste blood!' Shouts Ajax.

Resin snarls and charges towards me, scooping up a sword from the ground en route. I search frantically for a blade of my own but see nothing. I start to move to the side of the arena, hoping for a slight breeze or ray of sunlight to give me strength, but nothing. That's when it hits me. The arena must be underground, which means I have to rely on my skill alone to survive this. No powers, no sun to help me, just me versus the killer racing toward me. Resin grows closer and launches himself at me. His sword whizzes past my body, and I leap backwards against the wall, narrowly avoiding the attack. He is not going for the kill. He is attempting to maim me! He wants a show - he wants to chase a wounded animal first to please the crowd.

'Stop!' I shout, raising my arms.

He falters slightly, saliva dripping from his mouth. His lips not quite sitting flush with each other. His scars make him seem like a beast, not a man.

'Please, don't fight. You are not a slave. You are...'

Rocks and spit start to fall from the seats above me, the crowd booing and cursing. Chants of *kill him* fill the air. These seem to fuel Resin into a roar. He swipes at me again, his movements fast and fluid. I barely get out of the way. I run towards his gate, leaving him behind and frustrated at his inability to land a blow. He chases after me, his guttural shouts, making me run faster than I thought possible without the aid of the sunlight. Then I see it, a blade on the ground. I roll forward, grabbing the weapon as I pass and blocking his next sweeping attack. The crowd show their glee with a boisterous howl. Resin throws a punch with his other hand, connecting with my eye and plunging me into a world of pain. This skinny man punches like a horse kicks. I fall backwards, barely able to keep my footing. Resin surges forward, trying to catch me with a dropped guard. My sword connects with his again, and I once more avoid his hacking and slashing.

'Please stop!' I plead, yet it seems futile to a man in a battle frenzy.

He swings not for any vital parts but my wrist, catching me out and taking a huge slice out of my forearm. I drop my blade as the pain of the sharp weapon goes through my flesh. If only I had the sun. My father would defeat this man, but I do not know him. I don't want to harm him, but he wants me dead. I sidestep his next attack throwing my fist into his lower ribs, hearing a sweet crack as they break under the force of the strike. For the first time, Resin seems to delay. Holding his ribs, he looks at me like death would gaze upon a dying man. I back away and try to catch my breath before the inevitable happens. His panting turns to a frown, then shifts to an evil smile. It's as if he is enjoying the pain. I clutch at my forearm to staunch the blood flow. Thankfully the slice was on the top part of my arm. Nothing but muscle was damaged. Resin steadies himself before his next offensive. He starts toward me, picking up the pace from a jog to a run, I stand firm, waiting to dodge his blows again, but instead of advancing with sword in hand, he throws the weapon at my face.

The blade flies through the air, and I tilt my head to avoid it. I feel it crash into my skull as it strikes me above the eyebrow. The edge of the blade slicing my flesh, causing blood to spit from the wound and pour down my face, obscuring my vision. His fist plants into my throat with expert precision, throwing me off my feet and slamming me into the sandy ground below. Resin jumps on top of me and starts to pummel my face with his bare fists. Part of me is thankful that he has forgotten about the sword. I feel my life beginning to leave me - the pain threatening to render me unconscious. I drift into another world as my consciousness starts to fail me. I see the light, the one that people talk about when they have shaken hands with death. It overwhelms and blinds me, I can't see my enemy anymore, but I can still feel him smashing and clawing at my head and body. I start to go numb.

'It is not your time, Jacob.' A powerful yet soft voice says. 'You must not die here. You must fight. Now take up that sword and be done with him.'

The light disappears, and with it, the warm voice and numbness. My senses return to me. Risen stops pounding, shouting in a frenzy at the crowd, who respond graciously. In this moment of respite, I reach above my head, searching the ground for Resins weapon. I grab the sword, clasping it in my hand and drive it upwards. The point of it rams into the throat of the gladiator, cutting his chants short. The crowd gasps as Resin slumps forward, and his corpse slides down the blade and onto me. I lay there, the blood of my enemy leaking over me. I cannot move, but I have won, and I have survived.

The sounds of the arena fade in and out, the weight of the dead man on top of me eases as the guards drag his body off my broken flesh. I can no longer tell which is my blood and which is his. There seems to be so much of it.

'We have a victor! What a fight, people, what a fight. I haven't seen anything like this before.' The voice of Ajax echoes around the tiny arena. 'Let's hear it for THE SAMURAI!'

The cheers bounce around the arena. I feel that they would be louder if my ears were not encrusted with blood and sand. I feel two sets of arms pick me up and drag me back to the gate in which I came. They throw me back into the darkness.

'Well done, Samurai,' says the huge man again. 'I am Hacker. You have earned the right to know my name, and perhaps sometime in the future, you will earn the right to fight me too. Till then, friend, don't die.'

A different door opens, and the recognisable white attire of Ajax steps inside the filthy hovel.

'I knew you would be an asset, Samurai.'

'My name is Jacob.' I squeak, barely able to open my mouth.

'Your name is what I decide it to be, boy,' He laughs, 'and from this day forth, you are the Samurai. You will learn to love it, and in return, people will learn to love us.'

'I will always be Jacob.'

'You are a stubborn one, and that is why I know you will live through many more fights yet. Now, rest and heal, and your reward for killing Resin will be waiting for you. Well done, Samurai.'

Ajax leaves the room. I wish I had the strength to ruin that white suit of his, perhaps cover it in blood, not his, but the blood of the warrior I just felled, so he can go away and remember the man that *he* had killed today. His men pick me up once again and drag me out of the room.

I hear Hacker shout to me as I am taken away, 'You fought well today, friend. You bathed in the blood of another and killed an unkillable man. Rest easy, fight hard.'

I am taken to a bathing room. The steam rises from the hot water. The scent of eucalyptus fills the air as I am gently lowered into the soothing concoction of herbs. The slices on my body sting with misery as the healing water makes its way into my broken flesh. The guards leave me floating in the tub and watch silently. If only I could just lay in the sun for a few moments, all these cuts would be gone, and with them, the anguish they are bringing me. Two women walk into the room wielding sponges and blankets. They tenderly dab at my wounds, stroking away the blood and dirt, but not the memories of me having to take my first life. His face of ruin imprinted in my mind, those snarled lips and dark eyes, smiling blithely at me as he smashed my face with his knuckles till he could no longer tell where my flesh ended and his began. Still, I feel sad that I have taken his life. It is not his fault, but the fault of the man who put me here. The women keep cleaning me, they are beautiful and soft, and their healing hands remind me of my mother. I hope the village is looking after her and she them. What of Bipin? Has he stayed to help her rebuild? I wish I could go back there now, see my fathers face, spar with him and mother, enjoy her cooking and be hugged by them both, running for hours and chasing lightning dragons.

They finish cleaning me up, wrap me in bandages and walk me to my new chambers. They are clean but simple. Lit only by a single torch. I feel like this entire complex is underground. My bed is comfortable, and I have a small table with some food placed upon it — bread, fish and fruit. The meal is far superior to what I expect but nothing like the feast I had with Ajax. I chew it slowly, my jaw has almost seized up with the damage it undertook, and my eyes are so swollen that I can barely see anything. I fear tomorrow will feel worse, but for now, I am alive, clean and have food, so I choose to savour this moment before the darkness returns.

The morning comes and brings with it the smell of fresh air. Somewhere close by, a window or door leads to the outside. I feel the breeze stroke the tiny hairs on my arms, so I play with it, shifting the air around me. It comforts me. If only I had this when I was fighting Resin, I would have finished him much quicker, then perhaps I could have reasoned with him, talked to him before I was forced to murder him for the crowd's pleasure. I was so excited to see the city, but how wrong I was. I must remain focused, however. My father's killer is still out there, and I need to find him and get my revenge.

'How are you feeling?' I hear the voice of Ajax beyond the cell door.

'I have been better.'

'I expected more from you, boy.'

'I didn't want to kill that man. He was forced to fight as I am.'

'No, Jacob. He wasn't forced. He fought because he loved to fight and because it pays very well. He could have had anything and anyone he desired with the coin he had won. Now it all belongs to me, the spoils of war. So thank you for making me richer despite your theatrics.'

'Why are you forcing me to kill?'

'I am nothing but a businessman, and I saw potential in you that I have not seen for years. You made fools out of my guards, and they have a reputation that would strike fear into most. Yet, you appear and finish them in seconds. You have talent, and if you let me help you, then you can be famous and rich.'

'I want to find the Archivist, nothing more. Then return to what remains of my family and my farm.'

Ajax laughs heartily, 'You are no farm boy. You are a natural gladiator. You can be so great that you could defeat the Viking and take the top tier crown. Then, my boy, you will thank me. Women and riches beyond your belief will surround you. Then and only then will we be friends.'

Ajax has a stern voice, different from the day I met him. He seemed like a father figure then, but now I hear only a hollow man, driven by greed and power. A typical tyrant, like the stories my parents used to tell me. Tyrants that brought the almost complete annihilation of humans thousands of years ago.

'I will leave you to rest. In two weeks, you will fight again. If you survive, you will realise that your second kill is far easier than your first. Who knows, boy, you might actually start to enjoy it.'

I hear Ajax leave, his footsteps echoing down the corridor until a door creeks shut and the gentle breeze fades away.

The two weeks pass quickly, and I was able to start training in my room after a few days. My eye has partially reopened but is still far from fully healed. The purple and yellow bruising are still sore to touch, but nothing like the pain I had after the battle. If only

I had access to even the smallest rays of sun, all these wounds would be long gone.

I once again feel a breeze and hear footsteps walking towards my cell. I sit cross-legged on the ground, using this moment of calm before I am thrown in to face and kill another man. Could I try again to reason with them? Or will it end with my death? Resin loved to fight. That is all he seemed to know.

'Are you ready, Samurai?' Says one of the many Archie's within Ajax's harem.

'I am.' I bow and stand.

I am bound at the wrists and led out of my prison. I see the open door at the end of the corridor. Light pours through it, and for just a moment, I feel its warm embrace. I absorb as much as I can before it closes, concealing a slight breeze to elevate my power and warmth that will help to heal my wounds. We walk away from it and down some stairs into an underground passage. A few torches light the darkness, and the corridor seems to go on forever. I feel sick. A shadow looms over me, pushing down my shoulders and threatening to crush my spirit. I don't want to kill; I want to find my fathers murderer and bring him to justice. My mind wanders until we reach the same room I woke in just before my fight with Resin. Hacker sits in a corner, eyes closed and chanting a language I do not know.

'Sit. You will be called upon soon. May your enemies be slow or your death swift,' Archie bows to me and leaves, shutting and locking the door behind him.

I take my seat and wait.

'Welcome back, Samurai.'

I smile at Hacker, who seems to have finished his meditation. 'Hello again, friend. Have these two weeks been kind to you?'

'I have been relaxing, much like you, I imagine.'

'I had some heavy wounds from Resin.'

'The fact you lived and are standing after a fight with Resin is already some achievement. I know people are already talking about it.'

'But I almost died.'

'Yet you killed an ex-champion. Resin was one of the best, yet his thirst for killing held him back. He fought his way into the tier one championships, yet when he fought the Gladiator of Light, he was told to spare his life. Resin, in bloodlust, slit the fallen warrior's throat and was banished to fight in the lowest tier until he murdered a century of men. You were to be the hundredth.'

'Why would Ajax put me up against such a man?

'That is something that only Ajax can answer. Although I fear he sees your ability to kill and bring him a fortune, even if you don't yet see it yourself.'

'I don't want to kill anyone.'

'Yet, you must, I am afraid.' Hacker nods to me.

'Do you enjoy killing?'

'Never…'

Silence blankets the room for a moment. Hacker stares at the floor and sighs deeply. 'You must fight, and you must win, Samurai.'

The large doors swing open, and torchlight floods the room. Two guards unshackle me and gesture for me to enter the arena. I hide the breeze I captured by wrapping it invisibly around my waist. It cannot be detected. You would not see it, only feel it if you got close to me. It's subtle wisps flowing in circles, ready for my command. It feels like a child's comfort blanket. Its presence gives me a feeling of hope, even if it is only the hope of surviving. Live today, and find my fathers killer tomorrow. I must start to see each day as being a stepping stone to what I wish to achieve.

The crowds are doing their usual crazed cheering on my entrance. The familiar voice of Ajax can be heard booming through the battleground. 'Friends! We are here again. To see the unbelievable, to witness feats held only for the purest and strongest of warriors. You are about to bear witness with your lowly human eyes, gods disguised as men, fighting for the right to live and for piles of gold large enough to make a queen drop her pantaloons. Are you ready?'

The roar bellows, so loud the floor seems to shake. The people gaze at Ajax, holding out their hands as if he is their lord and ruler.

'I give you the Samurai.' Ajax screams in delight. 'Today, he will face the fury of the Dragon. You know him well, the martial arts master, stripped of his title for the murder of his pupils. Will his ferocity and savagery be too much for our new Samurai? Let the battle… begin!'

I allow the small captured gusts to drive me faster than should have been possible toward the middle of the arena, the gust pushing me forward just a split second too fast but enough to give me an edge. I see a katana laying on the floor, so I pounce towards it, rolling over and grasping it as I pass. The dragon favours a metal staff. We stand off, facing each other. His long black hair and beard tied into braids, he spins the weapon with expert precision, throwing his body around in a series of kicks and flips to which the crowd show their appreciation.

'Dragon, I am sorry for what I must do,' he looks at me somewhat confused. 'I do not want to harm you, so if you surrender now, we can both walk away alive.'

The crowd start booing and cursing. I glance at Ajax, who gazes at me angrily. He wants a show because the crowd demand it.

'Kill him!' The crowd shout.

Obeying the mob, the Dragon races forward, spinning the staff towards me at an unbelievable speed. I allow the wind to wrap around my body, shifting to his left with a spin and instantly call upon the gusts to wrap around my arms as I slash down with the katana, taking the Dragon's head from his shoulders.

I kneel before his body as his life leaks from his headless body. The frenzied mob are silent, as is Ajax.

'I am sorry, warrior,' I say to the fallen Dragon.

I stand and walk back to the doors, not once turning to see Ajax. The guards open the large wooden entrance and let me pass. They follow me into the room and close the door behind me, shackling my ankles and wrists for transportation back to my cell.

'I hope I don't have to fight you anytime soon,' Hacker chuckles and stands, 'My turn, wish me luck.'

Chapter 16 – The Show

I sit in the dusky cell waiting for Ajax. I know he will want to speak to me about today's victory. He will be pleased with how easily I finished off the Dragon, but my heart is heavy. This is not what my power should be used for. Yet, my parents had to use it to fight those who would oppose them, to keep the family safe, to keep the village from threat. I wonder what my mother would say if she knew I had to take innocent lives? Yet, if the descriptions are true, the warriors I have been facing are far from innocent.

A knock on the hard wooden door of my cell cuts my reminiscing short. It swings open, and as expected, Ajax walks through with his usual bodyguards and a couple of Archie's in tow. His suit gives off a pearlescent tone in the darkness of the room. It almost seems to glow.

'Jacob…Your victory was impressive.' His voice seems to be one of disappointment. 'Do you understand what a showman is?'

'I do, I think.' I respond.

'Well, although I am pleased with this victory, you don't need to please me anymore. You need to please them.' Ajax points to the doorway.

'I need to please the guards?'

'No, you need to please the crowd, the rabble, and the people.' Ajax exclaims. 'They are the ones that will bring you glory and riches, boy.'

'I don't want those things. I just want to be free to find the Archivist.'

'Do you think you will find one man amongst all this? You can have power here, and you can be the greatest warrior that lived.'

'I just want to find my fathers killer. Let me go!'

'Okay, let me put it another way for you. *If* you play along, then I will do what I can to find the man you seek. When you win your freedom, then you will find him and do what you wish. I can make that happen on the condition you play the game.'

He may be right, unfortunately. Ajax seems to know everyone, and he is both rich and influential. I will do as he asks for my fallen father's sake and because he is the only person I know here inside these stone walls.

'Okay, Ajax. I agree to your terms.'

'Good boy. Now let's make you famous and me rich. I have prepared a training room for you, and if you need anything else, please don't hesitate to request it. If you have a fondness for a particular type of food, let me know and if you haven't expended all your energy when the sun fades, just say the word, and I shall send you a woman, or a man, to make your evenings more... pleasurable. As long as you keep winning, I will keep providing. Just don't forget, make the fight interesting.'

'When do I get to fight next?'

'In two weeks, as always. So enjoy your time off till then, Jacob.'

If he wants a show, I will give him the best performance he has ever seen. The sooner I can be free of this place, the sooner I can track down that murderer.

As the time within the cell grows longer, I request that I sleep in the training room, to which Ajax, who seems pleased by my vigour, allows it under guard. The room is much airier than my cell, only deeper in the underground labyrinth. There is a constant stench of mustiness and mould, but my nose grows used to it. Ajax ensures that I am well fed and have a sturdy but hard bed to rest my aches and pains. He continually offers me evening company, but I turn it away. My parents never mentioned that side of life. I was always so focused on becoming the best warrior I could - I had no time for women.

My days have become merged. I wake in the morning, fuel myself, and start working on the combat stances and moves my parents taught me. I cannot run the sorts of distances I had grown used to, but this has made me realise that I was using the elements on a subconscious level for speed and repairing my body. It has become as natural as breathing, and now that I can't use it, my body feels the aches, it feels pains, and I grow to love it. The elements made me weak, and now, I must become strong again.

I don't train today. Two weeks have passed me by, and it is time to fight once more. This time, I will dance. My enemy won't know what hit them, and the crowd will cheer my name. It will be the best show they have ever witnessed.

My door swings open, the usual white suit-clad Ajax struts in with his guards.

'You know you don't need to surround yourself with those guards anymore,' I say to him, lifting myself off my wooden chair.

'You already look stronger, Samurai.'

'I already feel stronger.'

'We have a slight issue. I want your fight to last longer. Hacker had a small accident in training, and he cannot fight his opponent today. You will need to nearly lose, then we can up the stakes and make enough to cover both fights.'

'I have a better option.'

'Oh…Well, why don't you enlighten me.'

'Let me fight both mine and Hackers opponents. You want a show for the crowd. Let us give them something spectacular.'

'Your confidence has grown, my boy.'

'I have a goal, and if I get to it faster by helping you achieve yours, then let me give them a real show today. I have no fear or doubt. Today I show you and the world what I am made of.'

Ajax looks at me, both cautious and excited. 'Okay,' he says, unsure of his answer. 'Don't you dare lose, and don't you even think of dying. I have far too high hopes for you and a lot of gold on this fight.'

I bow, not once averting my gaze from him. He smiles at me, an almost kind smile as if he cares for me and not for the coin I am about to make him.

'I will make the arrangements. Don't let me down.' He turns and leaves me with his guards.

'Ajax... Can I please see the sun before my fight, just quickly, in case this day is my last?'

Ajax turns. 'You have one minute. Guards, shackle him and get another band to join you. He has one minute.'

'Ajax...'

He turns to face me once more. 'Yes, lad?'

'My blade, on the day we met. May I have it back?'

'No gladiator may have their own sword, Jacob. It is the rules of combat. Once you have won and once you have made me rich, then I shall return your weapon.'

I thank him and allow the guards to shackle my wrists and ankles. I can get stronger during the two weeks and use what power I can absorb to ensure my victory. I just have to make sure that victory isn't too swift. I am dragged to the opening I sensed when I was in my old cell. The sun pours down the corridor, instantly giving my body strength, and I feel my aches melt away. I feel reborn. They pull me out into a small courtyard surrounded by high walls. The heat here is intense. The sun burns wickedly above us, and this place seems to capture and hold the heat. What would be a funnel of warmth for these dungeons is a beacon of healing light for me. I lap it up, absorbing all I can and capturing some of the small drafts that manage to swirl their way in the depths of this open room.

'Your minute is up,' orders the bulkiest of the men attending me.

'I thank you,' I respond, smiling and bowing to the man. *Be kind to those who are unkind to you.*

You may change their opinion of you and become friends - my father used to say.

Their dragging persists, but I do believe it was a little less violent than the time before. Back to the underground we go.

The waiting room, as I now call it, is quiet. No Hacker to keep me company. I do hope he is okay. He seems like a good man. I listen to Ajax, his blaring voice through his cone-shaped tool, projecting it outwards and over the crowd. 'Today, we have a special treat for you. Our very own Samurai will be fighting not one but two opponents.'

I hear the crowd scream in awe, their bloodlust getting the better of them.

'Not only that but today, we have a special guest. Let's give a warm tier-three welcome to, Yerkasha!'

I hear the crowds wolf whistles and cheers, a very different reaction from the one they usually give to Ajax. Who is this Yerkasha?

The chamber doors are flung open, and the guards unshackle my feet and wrists. The usual heat and light pour in, and I stand at the entrance of the arena. I Look up to Ajax's usual perch, spotting the woman they call Yerkasha. Her stature is small, but her beauty is undoubted. She wears a red dress, the slit of it showing off a little ankle, but no more. Her auburn brown hair rolls halfway down her back. Her jade green eyes and small features give her a delicate look, but her stare is confident and stern. She seems to give the illusion she is both predator and prey. Her waist is tiny, as are her breasts, but part of me can tell that she is not fragile but exquisite. She turns her gaze to me, and a small smile appears as she whispers something into the ear of Ajax. I see him nod in agreement, and he nods to me.

'Let the battle begin!' He screams at the gathered mob.

I allow the sun to give me that little bit of extra speed; flashing forward too much would make it obvious and give the game away, but in a controlled manner, it can just make me seem very fast, but still human fast. I grab a blade off the ground and spot my two enemies heading my way. They seem keen to impress, especially considering they outnumber me. I shall use their overconfidence to my advantage, much like my father did when attacked by more than one. One warrior swipes a sword from the ground, and the other finds an axe. They slow the approach setting themselves up to flank me on either side. Warrior A, the blonde, looks agile. His body is thin but bristling with tone and muscle, reminding me of a cat. He is on his toes, like a feline ready to pounce, he circles behind me. Warrior B is of different stature. He is bulky and broad. His shoulders as wide as a doorway, and he wields his two-handed battle axe in a single-handed grip. I see what they are doing. Show off the big man and make him the one to worry about, enabling the quick one to rush in and stab me in the back. I have seen warriors try this while fighting my father - it never ended up well for them. I spin round and charge at the blonde, his eyes widening with shock.

I attack with a flurry of average attacks, letting him block each with little effort but enough to give the crowd what they want. I hear the heavy thud of his colleague's feet approaching. I can't get too cocky else, it could end in my death. I leap out of the way just moments before the axe would hit true, and stand to face both of the men. Their initial plan has failed, but I am sure it only feed their bloodlust more. The crowd are in uproar, wailing with glee and shouting in a frenzy. The bulky warrior shouts at them and pounds his chest with his fist, and the mob love it. I don't wait for them to approach me this time. I launch myself forward, this time towards the big guy. He swings his axe towards my skull, hoping to lift my head from my body in a single cleve. I slide to my knees and slice the warriors thigh, making him drop to one knee and shout in pain. The cut not deep enough to cause too much damage, but it will bleed, and the mob will delight at first sight of blood. The blonde jumps past his downed kinsman, attacking with grace and speed. I block every blow and spin under his last attack with the wind's assistance and stabbing my blade into his arm. Impressively, he keeps hold of his weapon and continues his offensive. These are strong gladiators. The big man is back on his feet, thrusting the axe menacingly towards me. His attack is slow and is easily sidestepped.

The blonde fires three quick strikes at me, the last of them slicing my neck. That was a bit too close for comfort. They push forward, lunge after lunge, backing me into a corner. Wry smiles appear on their faces. They think they have me, and that's precisely the game I wanted to play. I turn and run toward the wall at full speed, taking four steps up and somersault over the two. The crowd gasps in awe; they wanted a spectacle, and now they have one. I land and use the solar power to leap forward and gut the blonde, my blade thrusting through his back and stomach easily. He falls forward, clutching at the steel that has pierced his body.

The bulky man lets out a roar and swings for me. I duck out of the way, having to release my weapon, which is still sheathed in the blonde's body. He picks up his fallen comrades' weapon. The sword he now wields looks like a dagger next to the big man's physique and battle-axe. Now weaponless, I must think of a way to get to the big man's vital points and bring him down. His legs are weak. He has very little in the form of nimble movement, and a cut has already made. If a man can't walk, a man can't fight.

I drop to a kneeling position, pretending to be out of breath, giving myself a moment to grab a handful of sand from the bloody floor. The warrior approaches slowly, his face furrowed and covered in dirt, sweat and the blood of his kinsman. With the added power of the wind, I throw the sand into his eye, forcing him backwards screaming. I use his temporary blindness to my advantage, jumping up and kicking him in the jaw. He drops the sword, clutching at his face and rubbing his eyes. I throw another kick into his thigh, using the sun power to strengthen the attack. I hear his leg snap. He screams and falls to the ground. Before he has a chance to recover, I jump on top of him, summoning the wind to guide my fist and shatter his skull. At the very last moment, I trade the wind's power for the sun's, ensuring that my fist doesn't break when I connect. I hear a loud crunch as the man's skull breaks into shards. The big man stops moving.

The crowd stand in shock, giving a moment of silence from the usual roaring chaos. They look upon me with wonder and delight. Perhaps I went too far with my powers? They slowly start to cheer, building back up to the frenzy I have grown accustomed to. I look up toward Ajax and the beautiful petite woman, as she whispers in his ear once again, yet he looks unhappy with the victory. I wonder why that is?

Chapter 17 – The Lady

A week passes without hearing anything from Ajax. I have been confined to my training room for all of the days so far, with no glimmer of light or breeze. I wonder why he has not come to visit me since my victory against the two? Did I go too far? Perhaps I made it too obvious that I was using powers?

Steps approach my cell, but not the usual ones I recognise. They sound lighter, more elegant, the footsteps of a woman. My cell door opens, and the beautiful lady I had seen on the balcony with Ajax stands before me. She has come without a guard, which surprises me as she is so tiny. Even Ajax chose to always turn up with at least three.

'Hello, Jacob,' she bows her head. 'I must say you gave an impressive show last week. The entire city is abuzz about you, and considering you are only a tier-three gladiator, that is really quite spectacular.'

'Thank you…'

'Yerkasha,' the woman says.

'Thank you, Yerkasha,' I bow, my eyes not shifting from hers.

'I have not seen such a one-sided battle for some time, and you did it against two opponents. You are wasted here with Ajax. I have come to make you an offer. I have no idea how he *acquired* you, nor do I care, but he has told me of whom you seek. So, my offer to you, leave Ajax, and you fight for me in tier one.'

'What do you know of the Archivist?' I ask.

'All of my fighters *choose* to honour me in tier one. You cannot leave this place, so you may as well have all the glory of being a famous fighter than forgotten in the dungeons with the hordes of rabble,' she responds, ignoring my question entirely.

'Will I be outside?'

'Outside of sorts. You won't be able to escape if that's what you are hoping to do. The only way to gain freedom is through victory, death, or if I allow it.'

'What does it take to get released?'

'Victory or death,' she giggles. She seems so sweet and innocent, but how can someone innocent tell a man he is a slave until he kills everyone she chooses or dies?

'May I think about it?'

'Sure,' she smiles

'How did you get Ajax to agree to this?'

'We both work for the same people, Ajax and I. The difference is, I get the first choice of which warriors I want in tier one, well... that and I can be quite persuasive when I need to be. I can promise you a far better life with me, then you have here. You will get other gladiators to train with, and we have our own training area outside but within the grounds of my home. Are you not lonely in this place?'

'I am, but the outside is what I miss more.'

'You have an hour. Then I shall leave this godforsaken place. Choose wisely, Jacob.'

Yerkasha glides out of the room, pausing briefly to gaze at me from head to toe before shutting the door behind her. I hear the gentle footsteps disappear as she leaves the corridor.

Would tier-one bring me closer to leaving or escaping? If I am outside in combat, I would always have my power at my beck and call. I would heal faster, I would fight better, I could become a grand champion, but at what cost? The murder of many slaves forced to fight like I, who only yearn for the freedom I had only weeks ago? I must find the man that killed my father. Would my parents be ashamed of what I have already done to find his killer? Have I already gone too far to be redeemed? What would my mother say if I return to tell her the stories of what I have become?

I must find the Archivist; else, all this is for nothing. I bang on my door, and within a few seconds, I hear the clink of a guard's footsteps making their way to my door.

'What do you want?' He says

'I wish to see the lady Yerkasha.'

'Made a decision have we? Well, I hope you realise that if you leave, you are dead meat, boy. I have seen you fight, and I admit you are good, but you won't stand a chance against the tier one warriors. It will be a shame to watch you die; you seem like a good lad.'

With that, the guard walks back down the corridor and starts calling out.

'Made your mind up already, have you?' she smiles.

'I have, Lady Yerkasha. I will fight for you, and I will win for you.'

'That makes me very happy, Samurai.'

'I do, however, have a condition.'

'Oh, you think you are in a position to ask for conditions? You are a spirited one, and I like that.'

'I ask that you tell me something about the man I seek. Unless you prove to me that you will help me find him, then I will not come with you.'

She takes a moment, staring intensely into my eyes. 'Okay, although I am only telling you this because you stand to make me a lot of money, I know he is a collector of things from a time that no longer exists. How he acquires them, I have no idea, and I have never met the man myself. I know he lives outside of the city and commands a small army of men to do his bidding. I will send a message to him if you like?'

'No, I don't want him to know I seek him.'

'May I ask you then, why it is you seek him?'

'He killed my father.'

'Ah, it all makes sense now, a boy bent on revenge. I will make a promise to you now, Jacob, and I will sign it in blood. You help me, and I will ensure you have the information you desire.' She pulls a knife from her belt and slices her hand, offering it to me.

I drop to one knee. 'You have my word, Lady Yerkasha.'

'Jacob,' she crouches in front of me, 'Don't die, let that revenge fuel you. I can turn you into a god amongst men if you let me.'

For a moment, her stare changes, her eyes soften, and her calculating look dissipates from her beautiful face. She seems sincere and caring, which is far more than Ajax ever was.

'Let us depart,' she says, calling the guards over to clamp my hands together. 'I hope you understand why I need to do this, Samurai. I can't afford to have you escape. You just cost me a fortune.'

'My sword, please, lady Yerkasha.'

'Sword?'

'Ajax took it from me when I was captured. It was given to me by my father.'

'You won't be needing that, Jacob. Trust me,' she smiles.

It takes a full day to get to the house of Yerkasha, even by horse and carriage. It makes me realise how huge the city is. How can people live in this massive prison? No trees, no meadows, no farms or animals, just buildings, and the occasional mutt or street cat. I think it was cleaner in my cell then it was out on the streets. Yet the smells of food, spices and perfume fill the air and takes me back to the day I arrived at this strange sort of hell.

The carriage pulls up to a large building. Its walls are white and pristine, with a large iron wrought fence surrounding it. I see two men scrubbing at the bottom of the posts, ensuring that it remains it's beautiful white. It is strange. It seems that white is the colour the rich seem to desire, yet the city's most significant building is a grey so dark that it looms like a shadow at night. Only light from the windows flickering shows that it has people residing within it. I wonder what goes on in such a gloomy and dark place?

'Why do you all desire white?' I ask Yerkasha.

'White is a symbol. It is the light that shines on all those who are lesser. The white is supposed to give them hope.'

'You sound like you are trying to be a leader to the people.'

'The rabble need someone to follow, Jacob. If you think otherwise, then you are naive.'

'I may be naïve, but at least I am not pretending to be a deity.'

Yerkasha stares me in the eye, her softness gone, replaced by a wicked scowl. 'Jacob, don't act like you know what goes on here. This is far bigger than you and I.'

'Perhaps, but you always have a choice.'

'Do I?'

'Always, sometimes you can seem stuck, but there is always a route out, even if it is a perilous road to travel.'

The scowl disappears, her eyes once again soften. She is a beautiful woman. Her jade eyes glinting in the sunbeams that manage to penetrate through the window coverings.

'You are wiser than your age portrays, Jacob. But sharing that wisdom will get you in trouble. As with all my warriors, I hope you live long enough to be freed or love it enough to wish to stay. Till then, train hard, live long.'

The carriage comes to a halt, and the door swings open. A butler stands dressed in a fine black suit and hat, holding his hand out for Yerkasha.

'Come, Jacob, let me show you around.'

As soon as I exit the carriage, four guards surround me, and we make our way around the house.

'I'm afraid you won't get to see the house. That is not for the likes of you. Although I think you will enjoy your chambers.' Yerkasha points to the back of the house. The guards react in turn and grab my arms, taking me to a large building at the back of the gardens.

'I will see you soon, Jacob.' She smiles sweetly again and walks to the grand pearlescent door of her home.

Chapter 18 – Gengi

The building is far larger than I have imagined. A giant courtyard lies in the centre, giving way to a training area that dreams are made of. Every weapon imaginable lays atop of racks, wooden dummies are strewn across the sands and amongst them, men and women clad in nought but armoured leather trousers and strips to cover their chests. One among them is a beast of a man. Long platinum locks curling down his back and a golden beard enhancing his bronze skin and piercing blue eyes. He wields a colossal steel battle-hammer, swinging it like it's made of feathers. His muscles glint in the sun, and his biceps look larger than my thighs. He lays waste to his training dummy, smashing it to pieces in mere seconds. The other gladiators around him look half his size in comparison, yet they all have the bearing of a warrior.

'Oh, how lovely, Yerkasha has brought us some breakfast,' laughs a dark-skinned woman, who grasps duel short swords.

'He is a mere snack, Nightbane, not enough to satiate a teenage virgin,' a brunette woman hollers back.

'I don't know, Gora. He may have some skills to make up for his tiny frame. Perhaps he is good with his tongue? The smaller ones always seem to put in a little more effort.'

The entire crew of battle-hardened warriors laugh at me, all except the giant man. He stops smashing the dummy and places his hammer on the floor, much like a mother would place her babe, and stalks over to me. As he approaches, a large beaming smile appears on his face.

'Hello, friend. Don't listen to those vultures. They talk the talk but rarely walk the walk, and both those bitches probably haven't had someone touch their bodies in years. I mean, look at them. Who would want to go anywhere near them?' I have no idea what he means, but before I have the chance to question it, he places his hand out to shake mine. His grip is that of a veteran blacksmith. He could probably strangle a mountain lion single-handed.

'Hello,' I say somewhat sheepishly. 'I am Jacob… The Samurai.'

'Ah, The Samurai. I expected you to be…bigger.'

'Oh, you have heard of me?'

'Of course. Most people have heard of the small man that doesn't seem to die.'

I feel somewhat surprised by the small comment, but I think everyone feels small next to this man.

'Well, I hope I live up to everyone's expectations,' I say, trying to figure out if this man is a friend or foe.

'We have no expectations, friend. Just try to stay alive for longer than Yerkashas' last investment. She lasted just one outing before she met the reaper.'

'Only one, was she a terrible fighter?'

'Yerkasha doesn't deal with terrible fighters, but she was thrown between a rock and a hard place. She was forced to pit the woman against the strongest fighter in this top tier.'

'I can only imagine how fierce the greatest fighter is. Do you know them?'

The big man laughs heartily, clutching at his brick wall like belly. I have doubts he is a man. He is chiselled in places I didn't know exist. As his stomach rises and falls, his muscular frame ripples, much like someone who has thrown not a stone but a boulder into a lake.

'Yes, Samurai, I know this man well.'

It is then that I realise my mistake. He is the one. He is the holder of the crown. 'You are that man, aren't you!'

'I am indeed,' the giant bows to me graciously.

'But have you not earned victory, and therefore your release?'

'I am no slave, Jacob. I am a champion and enjoy the fight, the struggle and the rewards. I earn more coin doing this than I can doing anything else. I was born in blood, and I have no doubt I will die in blood, or at least that is what I hope.'

'You wish to die in combat?'

'Better to die in glory than die old and frail in a cold bed. I want to die to the cheers and the cries of all those whom I have entertained since I was a mere bairn.'

'Bairn? That makes no sense?'

The big man laughs even harder than before, 'A bairn is the word for a child where I am from, youngling. I was sold as a child before the memory of my parents were imprinted in my mind, and since then, I have never known loss. My life is simple, and that's how I like it. I step into the arena. I kill all within it. I get gold and get women. Simple and beautiful,' he says, counting his fingers to ensure he covers everything he likes about fighting.

There is much truth in what the giant man is saying, although my idea of a simple life would contain much more peace and harmony than his version. He reminds me of my father in a way. A man built for combat, a warrior, but I can't help but remember what else my father was. He was a protector, he was a husband, and he was a teacher. It makes me feel for this man. If perhaps he had been loved and nurtured as my father and I had been, would his path be different?

'Why the solemn face, Jacob? Are you worried about my soul?'

'No, not at all, you just reminded me of someone I once knew.'

'You have experienced more death than that of just the arena, I sense. Yours is a face of deep anguish. I understand that face, for I have seen it in the eyes of the loved one's whos partners I have ended, their sons and their daughters, or any who choose to lay down arms with I.'

'You feel no regret for them?'

'Jacob, I honour them all with the memories of the moments of brother and sisterhood we have shared. They die honourably in combat, and the great valkyries carry their spirits to the gatherings above the clouds. They sup with their ancestors and drink, and fuck as much as they please. Can you imagine that youngling? All that drinking, all that fucking, and no aching head in the morning. I would gladly die in combat to have that for the rest of time, but not yet, my friend, not yet.' He takes a deep sigh, gazing into the heavens above us.

The sun almost gazes back, and I feel its power all over me, wondering if he can feel it too. Not just the kiss of the warmth on one's skin, but the healing it provides.

'When I reach that place, I will remember those I fought, and the first round of drinks will be on me.'

This giant has no fear of death. He seems to embrace it and almost welcome it. How can you defeat a fearless man? I sadly realise that he will be the one I have to kill for my freedom, yet, I already know that I like him.

'So Samurai, you are a little rude to have not asked my name, but I understand that the first time within this fortress can be a little… unsettling. You will know me as Gengi, the Viking.'

'What is a Viking?'

'Ah, take a seat, youngling, let me explain some history to you.'

We wander out of the sun and into a large room, the smell of food bellowing out of a kitchen on the left-hand side. A funny-looking man with a big black beard, long enough to touch his sternum, looks over and nods to Gengi.

'That is our Arab,' proclaims Gengi as he bows back to the man. 'He is from a land long since lost in the great war those thousands of years ago. His fighting style is only matched by his skill in the kitchen. He can turn a couple of bunnies and some carrots into a stew that would make a king weep with joy.'

'He is a gladiator and a cook?'

'Oh yes, by choice too. He loves playing with spices as much as he likes swinging his scimitar, and people say that history painted his people in a terrible manner, despite being one of the oldest races known on this planet. He is a good man, Jacob. You can trust him.'

'How do you know so much about history?'

'Have you heard of books?'

Once again, I am somewhat taken back by his comment. Although his innocence at the remark is apparent, I feel like he has met many people who are not well-read. 'Yes, I have read many books.'

'Well then, you understand. One day I shall show you my collection of texts and history books.'

'But if you are so well-read, why do you want to fight? History has shown us that fighting can only lead to death and destruction.'

'From what I hear, you are a capable fighter too. Why do you fight?'

'I was taught by my father. He would explain that the ability to protect one's family and friends was of paramount importance and that he chose to fight so that those in the innocents in our village didn't have to. But you have no one to protect?'

'Ah, Jacob, but I believe that we are all placed here for a reason. Some can fight, some can talk, some can write, and some can lead. If something comes easy to you, then it is probably why you are here. Fighting is very easy for me.'

I can't help but agree with this man. He has a way of talking that excretes passion and truth. I feel somewhat drawn to him. His aura is pure despite his capabilities for bringing death.

'So you have never wanted for anything but a thrill of the fight? No wife or children, a farm or to settle?'

'My family is here, and now, you are a part of it,' he raises his gigantic hands, threading his fingers open and exposing his palms to me. 'Do these look like the hands of a farmer?'

'No, they do not. They look like you could strangle a bear.'

The giant man stares at me, then back to his hands, closing his fingers back to a fist. Returning his gaze to me, his brow furrowing, 'I hope I do not have to kill you, Jacob,' his brow relaxes, the smile I have quickly become accustomed to returns, 'Strangle a bear, I like that, youngling.'

I wonder if he could kill me? I fear that even with my powers, he will be a fierce opponent, and if I used them with a crowd watching, what would happen to me? I have to be subtle. I have to be quick. I have to be the warrior my father taught me to be, and I will make him proud.

After some more pleasantries and introductions, I have met the Arab properly. His name is Ahsa. The two female vultures I had met already, but following a proper introduction and now realising my reputation, they are less keen to eat me up and spit me out. One other, called Gloom, seems to keep himself to himself. He simply nodded to me at our meeting and went back to flailing the training post. They all seem competent fighters, most covered in scars with pain behind their eyes. All except Gengi, his skin untouched, his eyes as bright as the midday sun, only much bluer, like the deepness of a summer ocean.

We spend time eating, drinking and training. There are no noticeable guards, and the warriors seem to be allowed to roam freely. Gengi shows me to my quarters, they are plusher than my last abode, and although my door is locked, I feel less like a prisoner.

'Good night, youngling. May you dream of an endless cup of ale and a fair-skinned, big breasted woman,' I can hear the smile on Gengis voice as he walks away from my room. 'The simple things, Samurai, it's all about the simple things!'

There is something about this man that I am yet to figure out, but he feels like family.

Chapter 19 – Battle Royale

After a few weeks of getting to know the system here and the fellow fighters, I feel better than ever. Yerkasha treats all her fighters with kindness and respect. She and Ajax are like yin and yang. It would seem that she believes that a happy, healthy warrior will be more willing to win for her and have more inclination to survive.

We sweat and glisten in the hot sunshine. I attack my wooden dummy with a ferocious slice of a short sword - it is far heavier than my katana, but that will make me stronger. My Katana is long gone, lost somewhere between my capture into slavery and my being bought by Yerkasha, but I miss it. I am growing used to the hard training now, and within this time, my body has shaped into something harder and faster. Gengi has helped me with my training and has been teaching me about the rules of tier-one combat. Death is not a warriors choice but the choice of the winning warrior's owner. More often than not, the owner will choose death unless it is more politically sound to give mercy. It all sounds too complicated for me. It seems more about the power struggle of the owners than the fighters themselves. Yerkasha, and her champion, Gengi, seem to be very well renown, and since I have been here, I have witnessed him fell three more opponents. The man works the crowd very well. His charisma, looks, and skill combined make him not only a fierce warrior but one that is adored. Yerkasha knows it and uses him to perfection. He brings her money, power and glory, and they both love it.

'Good morning, my beautiful band of warriors,' Yerkasha glides onto the training ground, her perfect frame laden in a soft white dress with a high bodice that runs to her neck. Modest yet beautiful. A slight cut in the lower frills allows her leg and thigh to escape occasionally as she walks. I can't help but stare at her.

'Eyes to yourself, youngling,' Gengi whispers, nudging me in the ribs with his giant elbow.

I lower my gaze and stand to attention. She is a fair leader and owner, but I still do not wish to see if she has a less *accommodating* side.

'How goes the training my warriors?'

Gengi steps forward to meet her. 'It goes very well, Lady Yerkasha. The Youngling has added something new to the group, and his speed and agility will be much appreciated in the upcoming contests.'

She stares at me, perhaps to work out if I am worthy of the coin she paid. I am curious what would happen if I was to flee from this place? Would all the kindness shown to me so far be forgotten? Would Gengi slay me? Would Yerkasha order my death?

'It is time for our Samurai to prove his worth.' She says, keeping her eyes fixed to mine. 'I am entering him into a battle royal!'

The gladiators shift uneasy, and all eyes turn to me.

'You are the Samurai, Youngling. When you are in that arena, do not forget that. Yerkasha does not waste gold or time on those who are not champions.' Gengi says to me, much like a master to a workhorse.

'What is a Battle Royal?'

'It is a bloodbath,' Says Gora, shaking her head as if my demise has already been written in stone.

'Nonsense, Gora. A Battle Royal is a contest of all the owners' new blood. You will fight against another fourteen warriors,' our Lady states.

'You will fight well, and you will win.' Gengi reassures me, placing his shovel sized hands on my shoulders.

'Gengi, you have another crown fight.'

'Yes, m'lady, and I shall not fall. Your name will remain as pure as your spirit.' He bows to her and stands back in line with the rest of us.

'Prepare our Samurai. His big day comes tomorrow,'

She drifts silently back into the main house, her white dress trail leaving a snake-like imprint on the sandy ground. This woman confuses me. She appears confident, yet it seems like she should not be. She dresses humbly yet gives the impression she could fight to the death should she need to. She seems honourable and kind, yet she is willing to buy captive slaves for her own gain.

'Okay, Youngling, let us get to work.'

The next few hours see me trying various armour combinations. I go from wearing red leather straps to a full steel breastplate, so fresh and shiny that I can see my face reflecting upon it. Helmets adorned with feathers of all colours, making me look like a peacock searching for a mate. I look like a fool.

'May I make a request, Gengi?'

'You can always request, but that doesn't mean it will be listened to,' he responds, lifting his eyebrows at me.

'May I not wear armour?'

'Not wear armour! We wish to meet your maker so quickly?'

'I have never worn armour, and all of these make me look like a clown.'

The giant man bursts into laughter. 'Yes, they certainly do. It is your small frame. It does not suit you at all.'

'Well, thank you for making me feel more confident about it.'

'You are most welcome honourable Samurai,' he bows at me dramatically. 'I do not think Yerkasha will be pleased if you do not wear armour, and there is a lacking of time to make you a new set. If I allow you to enter the arena with no protection, and you die too quickly, she will be furious and cut off my manhood. Or perhaps refuse to allow women into my quarters, which would be just as bad.'

The giant laughs, but this gives me confidence. He seems not to take this whole affair particularly seriously.

'Okay, I shall pick these then,' picking out the leather straps and helmet.

'Strong choice for you. It will help you to remain fast and agile, like a gazelle. Just don't get hit by a hammer, okay.' He curls up his fist and pretends to hit me in the chest with an imaginary hammer.

We finish making the minor adjustments and head off to our quarters. I find extra food laid upon my pillow — a beautiful selection of fruit that makes my stomach flip with excitement. I sit at the foot of my bed, and it brings back the warm memories of days spent in my room reading as a child, remembering the comfort of my mother's hands on my shoulders calling me for food. I would quite often lose myself in the ancient stories of warriors and vagabonds, nature and the world as it once was.

The wind whispers to me of an approaching woman, her scent of rose oil preceding her footsteps, giving away that my Lady is approaching. The wind carries smell and sound these days, and all this time in combat training has helped me achieve a far greater sensory relationship with my powers than I thought possible. It has refined my abilities to fight, and I feel that my subtle movements and enhancements have become potentially even greater than my father's. I feel arrogant for those thoughts, but I consider how he would have fared within this gladiatorial world that has been forced upon me. Would he have killed like as I have? Did he only kill in defence? Would he have killed to entertain and fill the purses of those with no understanding or knowledge of Bushido?

'Hello?'

A knock on the door shakes me out of my internal thoughts — a soft voice pierces through the hardwood door.

'You may enter,' I reply.

A woman walks into my chambers, her clothing covering very little. Nought but thin strips of silk float off her perfect body and perfect breasts, her legs long and smooth, yet a face that looks too young to be a part of her.

'Lady Yerkasha has sent me to you, Samurai.'

'What for?' I ask.

'If this is to be your last night on our earth, she would prefer it is an enjoyable one. She honours you by sending me.'

'I don't understand? What are you to do? I am capable of feeding myself.'

The young girl giggles to herself, stalking her way beside me and taking rest on my bed. Her clothes drape off her, highlighting that she wears no undergarments this eve.

'I am yours for the night, Samurai. You can do with me as you please. She only asks that you do not damage my face.'

'Why would I damage any of you?'

'Some like it rough, some like it soft, but whatever way *you* like it, you can have it.'

It dawns on me that she means we can be joined physically.

'Erm… actually, I am a little tired from training today, and I… er… have a big day tomorrow,' I lie through my teeth. I don't get fatigued when I have access to the sun. It heals me as fast as my muscles rip.

'You want me to leave?'

'Yes, I think that will be best. I'd rather not be up past my hour of sleep. I fight tomorrow, and I must be victorious.'

The young girl looks noticeably shocked. She has a beauty that I have rarely seen, but it is not the beauty I desire.

'Are you sure? I have never been turned away before.'

'Apologies, I don't have the energy.' I hope she cannot see through my shroud of lies. The truth is, I have no idea what to do anyway, and I would rather not spend my night before combat, learning the ways of the woman and embarrassing myself.

'As you wish, Samurai. I will go back to my chambers.'

'Thank you, and good night.'

The young girl stomps off, clearly distraught by my rejection. Poor girl, I hope I have not knocked her confidence, she is a beauty, but that's the scary part.

I lay on the bed, thinking about tomorrow's battle. I have no idea what location we will be at, who my opponents will be, and if I will have access to the elements. I can only wish for it and hope that it brings me a step closer to the Archivist.

Chapter 20 – The Day of the Dead

'The day of the Dead?' I ask

'Aye, youngling. The day of the dead is a slaughterhouse. They haven't offered the crowds one for ten years. I guess the mobs must be dwindling,' says Gengi, looking slightly concerned.

'Don't worry. I have a few tricks up my sleeve yet.'

Yerkasha glides into the ready room. 'I hope you do, Samurai. I do not want my investment to die first fight.' She gives me a long exploratory look from toe to head. 'You look the part, Jacob. I have faith in your abilities, and I know you won't let me down.'

'I will not, Lady Yerkasha.' I bow to her, keeping my eyes fixed on hers.

She gazes back for a bit too long — the deep green in her eyes aglow with questions. I wish I could get to know her more. She seems to have elements of depth to her that she doesn't allow others to witness.

'Good luck, Jacob,' she says softly.

At that, Yerkasha leaves the room, her elegance trailing her as she moves seamlessly through the doorway and out into the courtyard.

'You must be careful, Samurai. Your gaze lingers, and I fear that she is noticing.'

'I apologise, Gengi. She is a fascinating woman.'

'I have never known her with a man, and unlike many of the slave owners, she has never to my knowledge taken a slave warrior to her bed, no matter how desirable he thinks he is. He smiles at me and winks. She is pure, and I think she wishes to remain that way.'

'Okay, noted my friend. I shall bow to your wisdom.'

He grabs at my shoulder straps and shifts them around, making sure that I do not slip out from my armour.

'How does it feel?'

'A little tight. Would you mind loosening them a little?'

'Tight?' Gengi frowns. 'As you wish, Samurai. Just don't go losing any limbs, Okay.'

As I am shuffled into the corridor, and at once, I realise why this is called tier-one. The route to the arena is a vast hallway of golden statues and weapons. The objects all with their own plaque stating who the warrior was or what the weapon is called. These are all very famous gladiators, each gaining freedom through victory or death but infamous for their battle prowess. As I approach the large granite doors to the sandy battlement that awaits, I spot it! *Senso*, my fathers' sword. I would know it anywhere.

'Please wait, may I see that weapon!'

'Death waits for no man,' the guard sternly states.

'Or woman!' a familiar voice responds from just behind us.

'Lady Yerkasha, apologies.' The soldier bows deeply.

'What interests you about that blade specifically, Samurai?'

'It is familiar to me, that is all.'

'Pick it up then, see for yourself.'

The soldier starts panicking and draws his sword. 'Lady Yerkasha, he must not have a weapon. You are unguarded.'

'Nonsense. The Samurai is of my band. He will never harm me.'

She walks over to Senso and picks it up from the fastenings on the wall. She delicately swings the blade around with some skill.

'I see you have some knowledge of blade mastery,' I say to my lady.

'You honour me with your words, Jacob. Alas, I have only learned a little from my warriors. My... company would rather frown upon me getting all rough and ready with a sword in hand. Here, have a look for yourself.'

She hands me the blade. The warrior guarding me looking like he may soon have a heart attack. The blade is light and swift and fake.

'This weapon is too light to be the sword I thought it to be.'

'Is that a fact?' She eyes me curiously.

I walk over to her, blade in hand. She is not intimidated by me in the least. She stands firm, not breaking her gaze.

'Drop the weapon, boy!' The soldier shouts.

I continue straight past her and replace the sword to it's home on the wall.

'Nothing to worry about here, she looks after me and I her. I would surely rather fight to the death then see her stricken.' I bow to my mistress and return to the guard.

Yerkasha follows us to the giant doors, walking just slightly behind us the entire way. Is this how these battles work? Are the owners told to enter the arena with their warriors? The look on the guard's face tells me that this is not normal.

'What are you doing, Lady Yerkasha?'

'Showing off my new blood, of course.'

'You are not allowed on the sands. It is too dangerous.' He responds, clearly uneasy at the thought that he would be held responsible should any harm befall her.

'No harm will come to me there. None of the other gladiators would dare to cause me harm. It would cost them more than just their lives.'

The doors shift with some sort of mechanical workings. The massive granite slabs thunder apart, allowing a flood of sunlight to burst onto my skin. I close my eyes and the sun's power surge through my body. The crowd is like nothing I have seen before. All the colours of the rainbow litter the viewing stands, and there must be fifty-thousand people gazing upon the sands. The roars echo around, and I see the other gladiators step out of the shadows and into the pit. Each one has a unique look, and all look very dangerous.

Yerkasha steps onto the sand, waving at the crowds, who jeer and chant in response. She steps up beside me placing her hand on my shoulder.

'Meet today's champion, my beautiful friends!' She shouts.

Some of the crowd cheer, and some boo, the other owners, however, look at her with disgust and disdain. They are not pleased with her actions. She blows a kiss and a wink to one man in particular. He is seated above a fierce-looking warrior with dark skin and long braids that reach down to his waist. His raven-like eyes stare angrily toward my Lady. He is a fat man, wearing a garment of stripes and a wide-brimmed hat to shade himself from the sun. He shouts something to the warrior below, who looks up to his master and nods.

'That warrior is called Xander. He was the tier-two champion. He will be your strongest opponent, so please be careful, and come back alive.' Yerkasha slinks off the sands and back through the doors and into the dark.

A voice booms from above. 'Let's get this blood bath started, shall we. Today we present a spectacle of grandeur for all you delightful, bloodthirsty animals out there. Today will be a day never to be forgotten, a day to satisfy even the most depraved amongst you.'

The crowd's roar in anticipation.

'In the north of the arena, we have the mighty Xander. A master of swords and untouched in both tier-two and three. Could today be his day? Or will it be just another day in the pit for him?' Xander nods in acknowledgement once again.

'In the east, we have Mercy. Aptly given her name due to her lack of it within the lower ranks. In the west, we have the infamous Shadow! The Assassin of Death. Tallying up over fifty murders before he had even entered the arenas. Rumour has it that it took an entire legion of Neodias soldiers to bring him to justice. In the south, we have Nymph. The crazed woman who has stared death in the face and made him piss his britches with fear. She is known for killing a man by gnawing out his eyes all the way to his brain.'

His descriptions keep the crowd going wild. He is a masterfully dramatic host, and I wonder how many of these stories are true. Nymph seems too tiny to be here, and she kneels and scratches like a flea-ridden hound. I must not underestimate any of these warriors.

'Lastly, we have Yerkasha's Samurai. Little is known of this newbie, but he downed the ex-champion Resin in his debut, then slew the dragon with a single blow, and if that wasn't enough, he mocked the terrible two alone and still came out the victor! I hope you are all excited... Let the battle COMMENCE!'

In mere seconds, chaos ensues. I stand calmly for a moment, just observing. My plan to make this battle more dramatic will work and surely please Yerkasha. I unhinge my armour, allowing its rigidness to slip from my shoulders. It is such a freeing feeling. I have no idea how warriors can fight with such bulk attached to them. Once clear of the red leather that I wear, I search the sands for a weapon. I flash-forward using the suns power, but not too fast to give away my ability. I find the closest sword I can spot. I take a moment to look up at the stands and to Yerkasha. I bow to my lady, her eyes of bright jade observing me like that of a hunter stalking its prey. I lose myself for a moment in her beauty, never have I seen such like it. Her softness and kindness on the surface, but a rebel and hard woman at her core. She breaks her gaze with a nod, and her eyes shift to my left.

A warning!

Out of nowhere, a gladiator screams at me, charging forward with an axe in hand. He has already lost this fight. To allow yourself to beserk during times of battle is to die. These moments must be approached with calm. Collecting your senses and observing all that surrounds you. I step out of his overly zealous thrust with ease, not needing any powers to avoid the strike. As I step, I shift my weight into his hip, knocking him off his feet and face-first into the sand. I stab downwards and slice through the man's arm, rendering it useless.

'Please, please show mercy,' he begs, and so I oblige, leaving him to bleed on the sand.

I take a moment to see how the rest of the warriors are doing. I see Xander finish two warriors with great ease. He dances around them as if a child was trying to catch a butterfly. Mercy seems to have got lost in pounding a warrior to death with her bare fists, smiling gleefully. The assassin, Shadow, quickly dissects two warriors with a dagger. He moves as the shadows do. No matter how fast they seem to shift, he is always with them, stabbing and slicing, till they all drop. A giant man named Thunder has already been wounded in the thigh, yet it seems not to slow him. He strangles the one whose sword remains in his leg until he stops twitching. Nymph is something else entirely. The woman who looks the size of a child is a demon. What she lacks in grace, she makes up for with sheer ferocity and fearlessness. She wields twin daggers with serrated blades, spinning and rending her way through three significantly larger foes. Each strike has such precision that all but one are murdered with a single move.

It seems to grow quieter. The crowd are starting to still their cheers as they all focus on what we six will now do. Xander faces shadow, Thunder to Nymph and Mercy, who is covered in the blood of her last poor victim, approaches me with a smile from ear to ear.

Mercy lunges forward, going straight for my throat. I allow her to miss by just a few breaths. She attacks again and again. I use the sun and winds to guide me to safety each time. She screams out in frustration and starts to lose her wit. Now is my time. She throws a huge swing my way, leaving herself open, and so I take out her knee - slicing just deep enough to prevent her from using her leg anymore. She stumbles, falling to her hands and knees. She stands, still wanting to fight on. She swings again, this time with far less grace. Mercy doesn't seem to understand that she has lost the fight. She drives the blade forward, and I use my weapon to shift my weight and disarm her with a slice to her hand. Spinning off the back foot, I swiftly move behind her, bashing her in the skull with my hilt, knocking her unconscious.

Xander has made swift work of Shadow, unsurprisingly, and I see Nymph chewing at Thunder's throat while he lays still on the ground. She looks up, and with a menacing howl, she races toward me. Her flurry of blows come swiftly. It takes all of my power to keep her at bay. A block, then a dodge, then a ripost. She seems to have an endless supply of energy and fury – her attacks are so swift that I cannot make a counter-attack. She suddenly spits blood into my eyes and kicks me in the nethers. I fall, doubled over. She leaps on top of me and thrusts her dagger into my neck. The pain is immense. I feel the blade sink into my throat, and she tears it back out, the serrated edge ripping flesh out with it. She lifts her arms for a final attack, and I push out my hips. With some subtle help from the wind, I throw her off and into the bloody sands. Bewildered, she rises, letting out another deathly howl. I instantly start absorbing the sun, healing my sundered neck. She steps forward, but without warning, Xander appears behind her, swinging his axe and severing her head from her shoulders. She slumps forward, her red insides leaking everywhere and polluting the golden sands with her vileness.

Xander turns to the adoration of the crowd; they think him the victor.

'Apologies, Xander. I am still here. The little witch gave me but a scratch.'

'What evil is this? I saw that blade cut deep.'

'I guess you saw wrong. Shall we?' I bow to the warrior, ashamed of having to use my power but glad to be alive.

This time I do not wait for the attack to come to me. I strike first and strike hard, using my power to rejuvenate my strength. Xander stumbles backwards from my force. I don't attack to kill. I attack for a show, smashing my blade into his, forcing him into defence. I keep repeatedly smashing, till eventually, Xanders strength goes, and he drops his blade. I didn't show grace. I didn't show skill. I showed strength. Something the crowds wouldn't expect from someone my size. He was too swift to allow any time for him to attack. I had already noticed the weak spots in his defence and wanted to utilise them. He is a master of attack, swift and sure, but his defence is lacking and leaves him open to my enhanced strength. *'Watch your enemy, learn from them and use it to find a peaceful end,'* my father used to say.

'Do you yield?'

'I yield,' he says, hanging his head down and dropping to a knee.

The crowd go wild with excitement. The battle royal is over. I managed to be the victor without killing a soul. I turn to face Yerkasha, bowing deeply. She responds by returning my bow. I jeer to the crowds, raising a fist to them as they chant my name, *Samurai.* As I peer over to Xander's owner, I see him whispering to a hooded man, handing him a small pouch. He seems to be taking no notice of his felled warrior. The winds whisper to me of voices, not of the crowd, but that of the man in the pinstriped suit. 'Kill her,' the winds tell me.

I watch as the hooded man weaves in and out of the bellowing crowds. Shifting like a river through rocks. An assassin!

I look to Yerkasha. She smiles at me proudly, clasping her hands together and waving to the mob. She has no idea of the danger. I race to the high walls, whisping the winds under my feet and jumping higher than a normal man should. I slam my sword into the wall using it to drive myself up higher till I reach the edge. I run along the battlements, and the crowd shift out of my way, screaming with terror. Soldiers approach, trying to cut off my apparent escape attempt. As one swings at me with a halberd, I flip over him with wind enhanced feet, clearing him and his weapon with ease. I see the assassin pulling a throwing dagger from his belt and taking aim. Yerkasha notices the commotion and turns to meet her assassins gaze; her face drops as she realises that he is there for her. He launches the blade toward her.

I must be faster! I release the winds and absorb the sunlight, flashing forward and catching the dagger in my hand mid-flight.

'Not while I live,' I say to the assassin, throwing the blade back. The dagger lands true, taking its rest in the man's forehead as he falls lifeless onto the stands.

'Not while I live,' I say to Yerkasha, my lady.

Chapter 21- Saviour

'If you were not the warrior I know you to be, then I have no doubt you would have made quite the career in acting, Youngling.' The giant man pats me on the back, his smile gleaming much like his golden hair. 'I have no idea how you saw that assassin, but I am sure as I am a Viking that the Lady of the house approves.'

'Thank you, Gengi.'

'I honestly thought you were knocking on death's door after that blade nicked your neck. It looked far worse from afar. A little flesh wound will not stop the Samurai, would it!'

'I guess I got lucky,' I reply, glad that I seem to have got away with it.

'You fought like a lion, my friend, and earned the right to be in the top-tier. You should be as proud a mother with a babe as beautiful as me.'

I smirk at the big man, and he laughs heartily in response. The door to the chambers shuffle open, and in glides the beautiful Yerkasha. She wears a dress that matches her eyes, only a deeper shade of glorious deep jade. The dress flows and caresses her skin, showing off each detail of her perfect body as the sun shines in from the doorway she entered, turning it into an almost translucent blue that matches the ocean on a summers day.

'Hello, my warriors.'

We stand and bow to the Lady in unison.

'Please, may I have a moment with The Samurai?'

'Okay, boys and girls, you heard the lady, let's get back to training.' Gengi leads them out of the mess hall and into the yard. The familiar sounds of swordplay and metal biting into wood is soon filling the courtyard.

'Jacob, I wanted to thank you for saving my life. I don't know how you noticed that assassin from the pit, but I am glad you have the eyes of a hawk.'

'As long as I am bound to you, my honour demands I protect you.'

'Is it just your honour? Or is it that you need me to help you find the Archivist?'

'You freed me from the grasp of Ajax and brought me hope of locating my father's murderer. All I have done is win you coin.'

'I guess that's one way of looking at it.' She smiles. 'I have something for you. Information regarding the man you seek. He is a collector of forgotten things — items of value that should never be found, as I have previously explained. I know he works for the same people as I and that they do not want him found.'

'How do you know this? Where is he now?'

'Unfortunately, I don't have that information. All I can tell you is that he is crucial to the ones that run this city. Searching for him is dangerous for both you and me.'

'Then you must stop. I cannot allow another to be in danger due to my own needs.'

'It is the least I can do for my saviour. *I* am honour bound to help you now.'

I bow to her. She is a good woman. Confusing but good.

'There is something about you, Jacob. You move like no one I have ever watched in the arena.

You seem lucky that the blades of your enemies don't seem to strike true when they have felled all others who oppose them, and you have the senses of a god. What is it that you are not telling me?'

'My father trained me well.'

'Hmmmmm, that he did.' She leans in and kisses me on the cheek. 'Thank you, Jacob.'

Yerkasha, my Lady, glides back out of the room and into the sunlight.

'I will always protect you.' I whisper.

Chapter 22 – Born a Warrior

'She was pleased I take it?' asks Gengi, who, even after an entire day on the sands, looked fresh as morning dew.

'She was.' I smirk at the giant man. 'She even kissed my cheek.'

'Jacob, come now. I always thought you were the sort who was pure of heart, not one to tell lies, even little white ones.'

'It is the truth.' I protest. 'She wanted to thank me personally.'

'Then she must be very pleased! I have never known such actions from the Lady. Well, I have also never known anyone to save her life, so I guess it's understandable. Don't go getting any ideas though, my friend, or a swelled head.'

'I would never. Plus… I wouldn't know what to do anyway.'

'Strike me down and call me a monkey! You have never lain with a woman?'

'I haven't. I am always training — no time for that sort of thing.'

'No time! If you were my child, I would slap you for saying such things. Jacob, Jacob, Jacob, woman are as close to paradise as we can hope to achieve in this world. The things they can make you feel... well, they come almost as close as the feeling of being a champion,' the big man laughs hard. 'I had bedded my first woman at twelve years old. Although I was probably already twice the size of you then, scrawny little man.'

The big man takes a seat next to me, passing over a cup of water and tears off half his loaf for me. He is always so cheerful and fun, this deadly giant. Even after all the death he must have seen and all the killing he has done. Yet, it seems strange that he would be so fierce and yet so gentle at the same time.

'How long have you been champion for?'

'Two years, I think? I lose track of it. As I said before, I like to live simply. I step into the pit, kill my opponent, or just harm them a little if they yield. I come back, bathe, fuck and eat. Ah, the simple life.' He lets out a huge sigh and sinks back into his chair.

'Have you always wanted a simple life then?

'Aye, for as long as I can remember. I think its fitting for an orphan not to want to achieve too much.'

'Why?'

'Orphans should not have hope. Their parents already left them and then sold them into slavery. Whats to hope for?'

'Yet you have proved yourself to be the greatest champion that has lived?'

'True, but if you think like that, then you run the risk of worrying yourself to an early grave. I don't care for my future; I shouldn't really have one. I care about the here and the now. Oh, and the next beautiful woman that I can swoon over.' Gengi seems lost in thought for a moment or two.

I leave him to daydream for a while, wondering what a man like him really wants. Surely it can't be his lot, fighting and fucking as he so eloquently states.

'I have had three owners, lad. The first was a ruthless man. He bought me to be a serving boy from a very young age. I grew exponentially in those first years and secretly trained with the guards. They all liked my sense of humour, you see. I soon became rather handy with a sword, axe and any stick they placed into my hands. By the time I was thirteen, I was besting them all, sometimes even two at a time.'

'So you were born to be a warrior.'

'It would seem that way. I don't believe in destiny, but I'm sure it would be that if I did. Anyway, let me finish my story, stop interrupting me,' he shakes his finger at me in a fatherly disapproval. 'The sparring didn't last. I was caught, and despite me thinking I was going to get in trouble, the shrewd man decided he could make some money out of me. As punishment, he threw me into the pit to fight a murderer. Let's just say that from that day forth, my blade has made people a lot of money. After that first fight, he sold me for a price one hundred times what he bought me for and is now living like a king as far as I know. My second master was more in love with me than anything else. He wouldn't let me fight as he didn't want to ruin his masterpiece. He used to make me stand on show, oiled up and nearly naked. Just at parties and gatherings mainly, or sometimes just alone. He never tried to fuck me, thankfully. He was a good man, or at least he was until he was stabbed in his sleep.'

'Who would do such a thing?'

'I know not, my friend, but I was both sad and happy.'

'I don't understand?'

'He treated me like a prince. He bought me many things, allowed me to sleep with the most beautiful women in the city, on the condition he could watch, and he seemed to love me. On the other hand, I had grown bored. I wanted to fight, and that is where lady Yerkasha saved the day.'

'She brought you back into the arena. Made you a champion, I guess.'

'Exactly that, Youngling.'

'Do you not want anything else in life then?'

'I love fighting, learning and women. What else would I do? I could be a farmer, I guess?' He prods me in jest, giving me a wink.

'So you will fight till you meet your maker?'

'Perhaps. Or maybe I will retire one day. Hoard my gold and go live by a river, away from this city. Get me a good woman and live in peace.'

This time I can tell he is being honest with me. No jest, no poking, just another long drawn out sign from the giant man. Ahsa drops a couple of bowls of his famous stew in front of us, and the conversation quickly comes to a halt. 'To the best days of our lives,' says the Arab, and we eat, chat and laugh till the day grows dark.

Chapter 23 – A Proposal

For the first time in what feels like an age, the rain is falling. I never thought I would say this, but I have missed it. We still train, only it is far more difficult, as the water pools up around us, creating puddles in various locations on the sands. Sparring can be challenging, but it does make for some good trickery. The odd flick of water into your opponent's eyes can give you a split-second advantage in combat. I have learned that there is very little honour in gladiatorial combat and that the most critical aspect is simply staying alive.

Although we all get soaked through and covered head to toe in wet sand, we all remain in high spirits. Each warrior has come out of their bouts victorious, and Yerkasha's fame has reached new pinnacles. With that comes glory and gold. And for Gengi, a lot of women.

Ahsa has had a particularly brutal fight against a woman called slavedriver. She used to work in the slave trade before pirates captured her. They traded females to the highest bidders and most ended up in local brothels. She was as fierce as she was angry. The irony was that she was the one who captured Ahsa in the first place. He was quite pleased to thrust his sabre into her temple, and the mob loved the poetic justice of it. Unfortunately for us, Ahsa took a rather gruesome blow to the arm, meaning Gengi was on cooking duty. He may be a champion gladiator, but his cooking skills are less than average.

'Samurai. Yerkasha requires your presence in the home,' one of her housekeepers stands at the door of our barracks in the rain. It's unlike them to be out here, but then I guess Yerkasha doesn't want to get soaked through like us. Her dresses are far too expensive for that.

I look at myself, covered in sand, sweat and rain with nought but my leather britches on. 'Should I get dressed first?'

'No need, she requires you urgently. I'm sure she has seen a topless man before, even one covered in muck such as yourself.'

They don't have much in the way of humour these housekeepers, but I don't think I would either if I spent my days polishing floors and making beds.

I follow him into the house, and he hands me a towel to dry myself off, else I drip all over the floor and ruin his handy work.

'Please follow me.'

The house is amazing — the halls wide and high, covered in beautiful tapestries which portray various histories and stories. I see everything from knights fighting dragons to the world tree from Viking history. All the doors that lead to other rooms are carved from oak but unfortunately closed, so I can't see what other wonders the house may be hiding. Every part of me wants to explore this place, but I must see my Lady first. No warrior is usually allowed to enter the chambers of their master, so this is a privilege in itself.

The housekeeper leads me to the end of the corridor, swings open one of the heavy oaken doors and points up the stairs that follow. 'Just go up those steps, and you will see another door much like this one. Knock and wait for the Lady of the house to allow you entrance.'

I bow to him and make my way up the spiralling stairway. Just as he had told me, at the top, another door waited for me. The intricate designs show a beam of sunlight streaming onto a female figure as she exits a dense wood. I wonder what story this image is from?

I knock and wait.

'Enter,' the familiar voice of Yerkasha's says.

As I prise the door open, I stand in awe at the vast library I have just stepped into. Books cover the walls from floor to ceiling - a ceiling too tall for reaching, so ladders on wheels scatter the shelves to help you get to the top run. It has a smell of old leather and burning wood. An open fireplace is to the door's right and is covered by a metal grate to stop any embers drifting off the pyre and into the books. The room must be hundreds of feet deep, with separate corridors all lined with volume after volume of history, novel and fact. What a wonder this place is.

Sitting by the large bay window sits Yerkasha. She is behind a small desk covered in papers and a little ink well. 'Come here, please, Jacob.'

'Yes, my Lady.'

'You like this room?'

'It is truly magnificent. I could lose myself for years amongst these pages. How did you accumulate all of these?'

'It is somewhat of a hobby of mine. I have a thirst for knowledge, and I have a lot of gold. So I always ask my people to bring me back a book or two on their travels. That is why I have called you.'

'You want me to get you some books?'

'No. I want you to accompany me to the market. The powers that be don't like their assets roaming the city. Yet, if I don't get to stretch my legs a bit, I start to feel like a caged animal.'

'So you will break their rules and put yourself in harm's way to stretch your legs?'

'I won't be in harm's way with you accompanying me.'

'I will need to put on more appropriate clothing then. I doubt you will want me roaming the markets with you like this.'

'I have prepared some clothing for you and a sword.' Yerkasha claps her hands, and the same grumpy housekeep enters the room. In his hands, he carries a blue suit and a sword sheathed within an ivory scabbard.

'These are beautiful, my Lady Yerkasha.' I pick up the sword and unsheath it. I give it a couple of swings. It is perfectly weighted, a sign that a master swordsmith has crafted it.

'It is a folded steel katana.'

'It is truly a perfect blade. Which hopefully, I won't have to use. I don't want to take these into my quarters. They may get ruined.'

'It's okay. We leave now. You may change here.' She turns around and gazes out of the window. 'Don't worry,' she laughs. 'I won't peak.'

I strip off as fast as I can, placing the beautiful new clothing on myself. I have never felt something as soft on my skin. It feels so delicate and light that I barely know I am wearing anything.

'I'm done.'

'Perfect. Now you look like my bodyguard. Both fierce and intelligent. Only a brave or stupid person would dare approach me with such a sight by my side.'

'It will be of little use as armour.' I say while prodding the flimsy material.

'That hasn't seemed to have bothered you in the past,' she says, reminding me of my little stunt in the arena. 'Right, let's go to town, shall we.'

We get into her carriage and start our journey to the centre of the city. The market is where I got myself in trouble the first day of being in Neodias. Let's hope today brings nothing of the sort this time.

'I couldn't help but notice your interest in the sword called *Senso*, Jacob?' Yerkasha asks.

'It is a beautiful blade, my Lady.'

'There are many beautiful blades in the gladiator's hallway, yet that one jumped out at you.'

She has trusted me with her life. Surely I can trust her with this. She is both wise and knows my cause. 'It was my father's sword before the Archivist killed him.'

'Your father's sword! Surely not?'

'Why wouldn't it be?'

'As you know, Jacob, I am a well-read woman. The Senso Blade is nought but a myth. The weapon of the Nephilim. The half-angels written into stories from the history books of a time past.'

I look at her, as honest as the dawn is replaced by the day. 'It was my fathers. The archivist has stolen it, and I must get it back.'

She places her hand upon mine. 'I am sorry for your loss, Jacob. If it is true what you say, then I hope to meet a Nephilim before I die. How did your father attain such a weapon.'

'He was one of the greatest warriors in the world. He earned it through combat, I think. I never asked him where he got it from.'

She doesn't look convinced by my words. She is far cleverer than I give her credit for. I glance out of the carriage window, thinking that my eyes will give away my lies. She suddenly removes her hand as if she had forgotten it was atop of mine.

'You will find him one day, I promise you.' She turns away and stays silent for the rest of the journey.

We arrive at the market place. It is abuzz with people of all shapes and sizes, rushing around buying products, selling goods and eating. The smells of the foods and spices bring back memories of the day I got in trouble here. The colours here are sublime. I sometimes forget that this place is so vibrant when I am on the sands. The people swarm toward Yerkasha when they see her, like hummingbirds to a flower. I stand in front, hand on my sword to ensure they come no closer. Instead of fear, their eyes widen like a full moon.

'The Samurai! The Samurai is here!' one of the folks shout.

The mob swarm around us, waving, shouting and cheering. A few of the females amongst the group wink at me and push their breasts together. I try to hide my blushing face.

'You are amazing,' One woman says.

'A true champion! When will you take the title off Gengi! I know you can do it,' says the young man at the front of the mob.

'Thank you. Thank you very much. Move back, please. For the safety of you all, I ask you to move back.' I say, with a stern voice.

They start to shift, pushing back and trying to make space. Within a few moments, guards make an appearance, shimmying off the citizens and asking them to go about their business.

'Lady Yerkasha, the marketplace is not safe for the likes of you.' The head of the posse states.

'Nonsense. I have the Samurai with me. I think I am safer with him than with anyone else.'

'We can escort you if you wish.'

'No thanks. It will only draw more attention. Come, Jacob, let us find some new books.'

'Would you mind if we visit a stall before we begin our scouring, Lady Yerkasha? There is someone here to whom I owe coin.'

Yerkasha follows me to the food stalls and into the famous smells that always make me hungry. After a minute or two, we find her. The old Lady I accidentally stole from on my first day.

'Hello, do you remember me?' I ask the old one.

'Have we met before Mr Samurai?'

'We have indeed.' I pull out a small bag of gold coins, handing it over to the woman at the stall.

'You can have my entire stand for that much, Mr Samurai. Hollys Dumplins don't cost that much.'

'This is what I owe you with interest. On my arrival at Neodias, I thought you were offering me food for free. I ate my fill of dumplings, and you called the guards when I couldn't pay. Please take this payment as a sorry from me to you. Plus, could I have six more dumplings?'

The old lady stares at me in shock. 'Why if it isn't the dirty, smelly thief who robbed me blind and escaped the guards. Oh, how I cursed your name those weeks ago. Little did I know you were the Samurai! Please forgive me?'

'It is I who ask for forgiveness. I hope the gold is useful, and perhaps you can find yourself a bigger stall. The world needs to know about these dumplings; they are delicious.'

I leave the old lady behind with a reciprocated bow. Yerkasha looks somewhat bemused by what I just did.

'You know you just gave that lady enough to buy a house in the lower quarters?'

'It is just gold. Plus, you really should try one of these; they are truly divine.' I hand one of the Hollys dumplings to my Lady. She sniffs it, unsure what to make of street food such as this. 'Take a bite. You won't regret it, I promise.'

'I trust you,' she says, taking a large bite. Her eyes light up, and her lips spread from ear to ear. 'Oh, by the gods! These *are* delicious.'

'I told you so.'

Yerkasha practically inhales another two. We chat and laugh, trying to ignore the awe and adoration of the crowd, and for a moment, it feels like it is just Yerkasha and me, strolling around the market as ordinary people do.

Chapter 24 – A Well-Known Stranger

A few more weeks pass by. I have been victorious in the pit another four times. I haven't been touched by the sharp edge of a weapon since the battle royal. My training with Gengi and the others has improved my strength and technique greatly. My father was an incredible master, but the fighting here is very different. You can battle without honour and morality. You fight for survival and for the hoards that watch. Gengi has helped me to become sharper and fiercer than I could have imagined. I have taken lives but not through my choice. Yerkasha has had to make statements to the other gladiator keepers and forced my hand, but I don't hate her for it. She has to play a role as much as I do.

Yerkasha and I have had more trips out to the market place, collecting books and eating food together. No threats on her life have been made since that day in the arena, and she seems to be growing in her rebellious nature. She is, however, more and more on edge. I have no idea why and she hasn't told me why, but I can't help but feel that it is partially because of the time we spend together. She is tough to figure out - could she have feelings for me, or is she panicked by what could happen if she and I fall in love? She has even given me a bedroom in the same corridor as hers, in case an attacker would sneak in at night. I am only allowed in it when it is my time to rest, but a room in the lady's house is simply unheard of.

It has been challenging to practice using my powers. I am never alone, except for when I am in my room. I feel like my connection with the elements is starting to dwindle. I would love the opportunity to train as I did in the fields with my father. Seeing how much more powerful I have become since training with my Viking friend. I need to stretch my wings and fly, but I cannot. I am duty-bound to my lady Yerkasha and must remain until I know she is safe.

My room here is too comfortable. The bed too soft, the fire always seems to be burning and a constant food supply. I think of my Kin in their barracks of stone and cots of hay and furs. It is unfair that I should be laden with all this comfort. None of them seems to care though. It is for the protection of our keeper, and so they seem to understand. I still spend my days with them, fighting and talking about our victories – getting sweaty, sandy and on occasion, bloody.

'Jacob?' says a deep voice from outside my door, at this late hour?

I whip on some clothing and ready my sword. I slowly pull the door open and am faced with a silhouette of a torso as big as the doorway. 'Bipin! How did you get in the house?'

'Jacob, you insult me. You know if I do not wish to be seen, then I am not.'

I am always surprised by his ability at stealth despite his stature.

'Come in quickly.' I shut the door and point to the seat over by the constantly burning fire. 'What in the gods brings you here?'

'Good news and grave news, young Nephilim.'

'Oh, please tell me! What of my mother is she well?'

'Your mother is doing well, Jacob. The town has rebuilt her home, and the farm is back to the way it was. My only fear is that she continues to shy away from her summoning.'

'I don't understand?'

'She is Nephilim, Jacob. She and your father were protectors of this world. Born for the sole reason of helping prevent the humans from destroying each other.'

'Have I been summoned too?'

'That is why I am here. You have lingered too long in this place. It is time to leave. You have a bigger purpose than this, and as your watcher, I must set you back on your path.'

'I don't want to leave. I have friends here, and I have to protect the lady of the house. I have responsibilities in this place and to them.'

'Do you not feel it, Jacob? Do you not feel the shadow looming on the horizon? That when the sun sets, it brings with it a feeling of dread.'

'I have not felt anything but the rush of battle and…'

'And you have fallen for this Lady of the house.'

'No, I haven't. We could never…'

'I cannot understand fully, young Nephilim. You have been gifted the emotions of humans, much like your parents. You can love, I can not. My job is a solitary one, but an important one. I must keep watch over this world - my eyes and ears see and hear all, yet I cannot trifle with humans' needs. That is why we need you.'

'Need me to what?'

'We need you to get Senso back and take it for your own.'

'And I intend to. But I have to protect Yerkasha first.'

'If that blade gets into the hands of the wrong people, then it will lead to more death, more than you can ever imagine. The sword must only be wielded by the pure of heart. Should an evil man take up the Nephilim's sword, then it could be disastrous. The power it holds needs to be contained.'

'Then why don't you search for the man, sneak in, and steal it back yourself?'

The watcher stares into the fire with no response to what I have asked him. Just gazing, watching the flames dance around the logs, the heat kissing the wood and turning it into an ashen grey.

'Jacob, this shadow I feel, will bring fire and death. I have felt it before you see. Not as concentrated as I feel it now, but in the hearts of men a few thousand years ago. When I felt it all those years ago, it was before the end times. Before the great war and the almost complete annihilation of the human race. Like this fire, it will turn the ground to ash. All that you love will be dead.'

'Then let us chase the shadow? You are a watcher. You must know where it is?'

'That is the problem, Jacob. I cannot see the shadow. I can only feel it, which means it is not of this world but mine.'

'You still don't answer my question. Why can't you sneak in and snatch it from them? If you do not want to be seen, then you won't be, right?'

'I cannot meddle in the affairs of humans. If I do, then a watcher I will no longer be, and I will be summoned back from whence I came.'

'Do you always speak in riddles, Bipin?' I say to the watcher, who is clearly sensing my frustrations.

'There will be a time for you to leave this game you are playing, Jacob. When the time is upon you, you will feel it. Be ready.'

Bipin rises from his chair, doing his usual gazing into my soul before he exits the room and into the darkness beyond. I have no doubts in my mind that I will see him again sooner rather than later, and as much as he frustrates me, I can't thank him enough for watching over my mother and ensuring her safety in my absence. I would say he has a good heart, but I'm not sure he has one. I don't understand why he cannot meddle and why he can feel and sense things I cannot. He has great power. He is lucky to have no emotion; it would be most frustrating being given the gifts he has, only to be told that he cannot use them. I wonder if he had parents or siblings? Or was he simply a creation? I have so many questions about this enigma of a man.

Chapter 25 – Till Death Do Us Part

I can feel the seasons changing during training today. The sun is a little less fierce, and grey clouds loom in the not too far distance. They start to look like mountains on the horizon. Big, dark and full of beautiful rain. Finally, I will have a better chance to train with the subtleties of the raindrops during combat. I didn't have much opportunity to learn that aspect of the elements before my father was taken from me, but I will now be able to after all these months away.

I face Gengi, my opponent, as usual during these days on the sands. His colossal hammer in his even bigger arms threatening to shatter my confidence and skull if I am not careful. You would think he would be slow, swinging something of that size around the battlefield, yet he wields it like I would a katana.

'Are you ready, Youngling?'

'Of course, Old Viking,' I sneer in an attempt to dampen his spirits through jest.

I don't think anything could dampen the spirit of Gengi. He is such a deep thinker and an educated man, yet, he only wants for a simple life of women, winning and wondrous words. You have to hand it to him; if any man I have met so far will find enlightenment, it would be he.

Before we have the chance to attack each other, Yerkasha does her usual gliding towards us. Something is different. She doesn't wear her familiar gentle looks and sweet yet firm demeanour.

'Gengi, Jacob,' she bows to us both, and we both respond in kind.

'My Lady, is everything okay? Do you require us to beat some sense into those who upset you?' says Gengi, who holds up his massive hammer.

'If only it were as simple as that, Gengi. Thank you for your efforts to lift my mood,' her frown retracts for a moment but soon returns as she looks at us both. 'I have grave news. Something has occurred that is not in my control. The people are calling for you both to fight.'

'We do fight every week?' I respond.

'I mean you to fight each other. To the death.'

Gengi and I look at each other, and for the first time, I see the big man look serious.

'The powers that control us all have requested that it happens. It will be the biggest and most lucrative show they will have ever put on. I am so sorry. I wish I could release you, but it would mean my end.'

'What if I simply run away?' I say, not knowing if I should be comforting her or holding her. We have become so close, but I cannot overstep my position, especially in front of the others.

'Jacob, these people are not foolish. I am afraid that if you run, they will know I have allowed it. They already warn against me being too close to my gladiators, yet you have all become so much more than just warriors in the sand. You have become my friends.' She bursts into tears, her usual calm and reserve have left her entirely, yet even as the tears flow from her eyes, she remains the most beautiful woman I have ever seen. 'I do not wish to see any of you die.'

'There must be a way,' Gengi responds. 'We are a smart collective. I'm sure we can come up with something?'

'My champion,' she holds Gengi's hand, and her red eyes meet his. She turns to face me, 'My... my friend.'

She leaves us, sobbing back to her home.

'Well, Jacob. It would seem that you and I are to cross weapons for real,' the giant man says to me, placing his hand on my shoulder with a grip of steel.

'I don't want to. You are my friend, my kin. I will run. I will get back onto my quest and hope that you can protect Yerkasha.'

'Quest?'

'Yes, Gengi. I am here to find my fathers blade, the *Senso* sword. It was stolen by the man that killed my father, using a deadly weapon that I intend to find, and destroy.'

'I knew there was something about you. You fight for reason, not just for survival. I could tell, but your business is yours alone, and so I didn't intrude.'

'You are a good man, Gengi.'

'I know, I know,' he says, laughing at me and shaking me like a ragdoll with his arm still on my shoulder. 'If you run, Yerkasha will surely die.'

I take a seat on the sands, contemplating what move I must make. I do not want to kill this man, and I don't wish Yerkasha to suffer.

'Let yourself worry no longer, Youngling. This fight we must have, will see you a champion.'

'That would mean your death.'

'So be it. You have a quest, and you are in love. I have always felt like you had a purpose greater than this. I will not be the one to put an end to it.'

'I will not kill you! You are my only friend.'

'But you must anyway. With my death, you will be the champion. The powers that cover this place in shadow will be happy, and Yerkasha, our lady, will be safe. Your purpose is greater than mine, and I have had a good life. Why not end it while it is still good. It is better to die by the blade of a friend, then old, decrepit and lonely in bed without the ability to get hard and please a woman anymore,' he laughs much like I imagine a dragon would roar. He is a man that manages to make even the purest thoughts sound like they belong in the gutter.

'You are a good man, Gengi. I do not want this.'

'You have no choice. My mind is made. I do want some answers, though?'

'Answers? To what?'

'Why you have powers?'

I look at the man, words stolen from my lips for a moment. I stare as he smiles widely.

'You think I was born yesterday? I am a warrior and have been my entire life. You heal too quickly, and I know the dagger of Nymph was a mortal wound. God only knows how many times I have done that to someone.'

'I… why have you not asked me before?'

'Your business is your own, as I just spoke. But as you will soon kill me, I feel I deserve to know.'

This man acts like a fool from time to time, but he is far sharper than I imagined. The only worry I have now is if anyone else amongst the crowds noticed it too. Would more warriors come after me? Is this why they want us to fight?

'You had better sit, Gangi. This will be hard to believe.'

We sit and chat for hours, and I explain everything to him. I tell him of my powers, how they manifested on my birthday, the lightning dragon, and how my father died. He had read about Nephilim before but looked quite surprised that they are real, but instead of fear, the Viking shows great excitement and pleads for a show of my power. I swirl the wind around my fingers, firing it out at the big man, which he finds hilarious. I cut myself with a dagger on my finger then absorb the sun to make it heal in seconds. Finally, I tell him about my mother and Bipin the watcher. Which further underlines my need to be victorious on the battlefield against him. He says that my mother needs me, and by the sounds of things, the whole world might too.

'Jacob, you must win, and you must leave. I fear that you have lingered too much here already — the blade sounds of great importance. Your friend

Bipin sounds wise, and you cannot allow love to blind you or hold you back, especially the romantic love you have, which is very cliché. It could almost be a tale written in a book. You are Nephilim. You are special, don't waste your life here in the pits. Magical beings should not be caged, my friend.'

'But I don't want you to die. You are too good a man to die in a place such as this. I want you to fulfil your dream of a house by the river with a voluptuous woman that makes you happy.'

'I have had enough women to make a king blush, Jacob. No need to worry about that. I will die a warrior. I will die like the Vikings of history, and I will journey to the afterlife in search of Valhalla and my ancestors from ages past. I will find out if all the stories are true if Odin lives or if Thor's hammer is as beautiful as mine. And if they are not true, well, I will just come back and haunt you till you find the power to bring me back.'

I smile at my friend. The fiercest warrior I know, with the softest heart.

'My life is yours, brother. But let us give them a show to remember,' he says.

Chapter 26 – It's Better to have Loved and Lost

The night before my fight with my friend and brother, Gengi, is upon me. I can't help but feel horrified at the position I am in. If I run, I kill the woman I love, and if I fight, I kill my only true friend and one of the most incredible people I have ever met: a true champion, warrior and Viking. I sit in my room, within the house of Yerkasha, thinking about how perhaps I should have stayed and helped my mother rebuild. What's the worst that could have happened? The sword would get into the hands of someone evil, and they take over the world? Perhaps then my entire family would have died, not just my father. Maybe all of this is destiny, or punishment for my parents having me in the first place, against the will of the gods and watchers? I don't know why this is happening to me. All I know is that I don't want to do it, how can I slay my friend.

I hear a knock on my door. No doubt this is Bipin once again sneaking into the house to tell me that I must leave and find the sword. I am, however, surprised to find Yerkasha standing before me.

'I want to speak to you alone, Jacob. I... I hope I am not disturbing you.'

'No, no, please come in.' I say, ushering her into my room and my forever burning fireplace. 'What can I do for you, my Lady?'

'Jacob, I want to personally apologise to you for the predicament I have placed you in. I hope you understand that it is not within my power to change what has come to pass. Yet I feel completely responsible for what is about to happen.'

'I know what it feels like to be a slave to something, My Lady.'

'Please, just Yerkasha. Both Gengi and you are far better people than I could ever be.'

'You treat us very well, you are a good person, and I won't have anyone say otherwise, else they feel the cut of my blade.'

She smiles sweetly at me, stepping a little closer. 'You are special, I can feel it, and the world can see it when you fight.'

I suddenly feel like the whole world knows I am Nephilim.

'I am sorry I make you kill. I know that you hate to take a life when it can be spared,' she steps closer again, so close I can see her perfect jade eyes glinting with the fire behind us. My cheeks start to turn red. Thank the gods that it's dark in this room.

'I have lied to you. I want you to know I am sorry about that too,' she breaks her gaze, looking to the floor. 'I have known the whereabouts of the Archivist for a while now.'

'Why have you not told me?'

'I… I didn't want to lose you,' she leans in, her lips graze my own. I feel her breath against mine, and my heart threatens to burst out of my chest.

For a moment, we stay there, lips touching. Her hand strokes my face, and I wrap my arms around her. For the first time, I feel her body close to mine. All of her perfect curves pressed against me, my cheeks now burning with both my shyness and my desire. How can I please a woman such as she? I have no experience in the ways of love, only with sword and steel.

She pulls away, 'We can't do this, can we? It may be your last day alive; how can I go on knowing your death is my fault?'

'It is not your fault, Yerkasha. It is the fault of the puppet masters that deny you everything for the sake of themselves and their business. You did bring me here, but I chose to stay because of you.'

She reluctantly peels herself away from me, sits on the stool close to the fire, her hands covering her face. 'The Archivist is a week ride south of here within the snowy mountains. He owns a large piece of land that is fortress-like. Within it, he stores secrets and items from the past. He has an army within the walls, an army with weapons the like you have never seen. Machines of death, the whisperers say, made from steel and breathe fire like dragons. Please do not rush to him. There is no point surviving the trials that await you tomorrow, just to be killed a week later at the hands of a man such as he.'

'I will be victorious. And once I am, I will return for you.'

'You are naïve, Jacob. I cannot be with you. A lady of a gladiatorial house, with one of her gladiators? It would be the end of me for sure.'

'Then, I shall take you away from here?'

She stands again, running over to me and taking me into her arms. 'You are already my hero, Jacob. But I cannot leave this place. I am more of a slave than you. Being a champion can release you from the companies grasp, but I am stuck here till my death, be it through age, illness, or if they simply do not find me useful anymore.'

She kisses me. She kisses me passionately and for the longest and most beautiful moment of my life. My heart feels as though it will burst out of my chest at any moment. How can it be that a woman as perfect as she would fall for a man like me? She starts to undo the buttons on my shirt but grows impatient and lifts the remainder of it over my shoulders. She has seen me wearing less, but this is very different. She gazes upon my body, biting her bottom lip and strokes my chest with her hands. She grabs my hands, placing them onto her, making me undo her dress.

'I… have never lain with a woman before.'   I admit.

She smiles softly again, yet I see a fire inside her like never before, her lust giving her away and telling me all I need to know. 'Don't worry, Jacob.'

She takes my hand and leads me to the bed. She turns to me, dropping her dress to her feet. The moonlight shines through my window, making her beautiful pale skin glow. For that moment, she seemed not to be human; her beauty surpassing anything I have laid my eyes on before. Her nakedness so pure and perfect, yet filling me with desire. She beckons me over, and so what am I to do but obey my mistress.

We lost ourselves in passion, her breath on my neck driving me crazy. For the first time in my life, I feel that all of my control over this world and myself have been relinquished, passing it over this woman, forever, my love. She removes my trousers, making me as naked as the day I was birthed. My fear dissipates with my growing need for her. She takes control of me, laying me down on the bed and kissing my body, working her way down my chest and stomach, kissing my hips and then taking me in her mouth. I am lost in another world — this beauty, this lady, making me feel like I have never felt before. She stops just before I finish, climbing back up my body and laying on her back. I try my best to emulate what she did, kissing her breasts and taking them into my mouth, listening to her moans. I bite her thighs, making her back arch and listen to her giggle. My tongue touches her between her legs, and I feel her tense. She grabs my hair and pushes my head closer. Her legs tightening around my head and neck.

'Here,' she tells me, touching herself.

Where her fingers guide, I put my tongue. Her writhing is letting me know that I am doing it right. She moans harder, her breath more frantic, making me want more. Suddenly she lets out one final huge moan, her whole body shivering.

'I want you, right now, Jacob.'

She sits up and forcefully pushes me back onto the bed, climbing on top of me. She takes me and slides me inside her, both our bodies connecting and in harmony. She moves herself up and down, her hands on my chest. It feels like nothing I could have ever imagined, even in my wildest dreams. The moon catches her body again, her breasts small yet perfect, her eyes closed as she sighs with pleasure. I grab her delicate waist and start to drive myself forward, which makes her moan harder once again. We move faster and faster, pushing and squirming; our bodies entwined, sweaty and moving as one. She pushes me back down, shifting her body backwards and forwards, each time bringing me closer until I cannot hold it any longer. I explode inside her, my legs paralysed, my body shaking, and my heart pounding harder than ever before.

She slides off me, laying on the bed beside me, taking my hand in hers and holding it to her breast.

'Never forget me, Jacob.'

'I could never forget you. You have my heart, my soul, my everything.'

Chapter 27 – The Great Shall Fall

Sitting, waiting for the inevitable is terrible. I don't want any of this. I should have escaped as soon as Yerkasha bought me. Now I find myself in the same room, in the same arena, about to kill my friend.

A knock on the door jolts me out of my daydream.

'It is time,' a guard says as I open the door. He nods to me in respect, 'My coin is on you, Samurai. May the gods give you wings.'

'Thank you.'

I step into the corridor. The same hall full of weapons, armour and statues of great warriors. I walk past the fake *Senso* blade. It reminds me of why I am here and that I have a higher purpose than this. It doesn't make me feel any better about having to slay my friend. He has been a light in this dark time for me; he is a good man.

I stand at the double doors, the sounds of the crowds piercing through the heaviness of them. It sounds like an army out there, chanting for their Viking and their Samurai. The doors fling open, and the mob roar like I have never heard before, the very sands I step onto, vibrating with the noise of it. On the opposite side of the arena, I see him: his vast stature, long blond hair, and shining steel breastplate. They have spared no expense. My chosen leather armour is both light and beautiful. The intricately worked images on it, depicting both Gengi and me, fighting against each other, lightning striking around us and fierce beasts standing on the edges of the arena watching us battle. It is a work of art. Yet soon, it will be covered in the blood of my kin.

The crowd simmers down, silence enveloping the arena. I hear nothing but my own beating heart as Yerkasha walks to the edge of the battlement overlooking us. Her eyes red, but her poise commanding.

'Today, we bear witness to one of the greatest battles in history. A war between two of the finest warriors the world has ever produced. The Samurai versus the Viking!' She shouts to the crowd, and they love it. They erupt with roars of glee and anticipation of what they are about to witness. 'Alas, my friends, this is not a time to rejoice.' The mob settling, confused by what the Lady is saying. 'What we are about to see is a sin. These two incredible men fighting to the death for what? For your joy? For coin? A waste of magnificence.' Her tears once again trailing down her face.

I gaze about the crowd, the look of shame plastered all over their faces. What is she doing? Surely she has taken this too far this time. The other slave owners are already whispering to each other, puffing out their chests in disarray. I try to catch a whisper or two on the wind, calling for the breeze to tell me what they are saying.

'She must die. She is too much. She is arrogant. She must perish.'

'Yes, yes. Feel shame for this want. The blood of innocents spilt across the sand for your amusement. Alas, for we are all savages,' she pauses for a moment, staring into my soul and ripping my heart from my ribcage, 'let the battle begin!' She shouts.

Suddenly there is nothing, just Gengi and me. I absorb the sun making myself a little too swift for a human, grabbing a dusty blade from the pit floor. Gengi searches frantically for a hammer, but the only one I see is near me.

'Come, claim your weapon, mighty Viking,' I say, bowing to the big man.

He strolls over, his famous smile beaming over to me as he picks up his weapon of choice.

'You are too honourable, Mr Samurai, Sir.'

Even now, in the face of death, Gengi's jests with me, bowing dramatically and deeply, giving me a wink. We start to circle each other, neither of us wanting to strike first.

'Don't kill me too quickly, Youngling. The crowd want a show, although I do feel Yerkasha has perhaps broken their spirits somewhat with that little speech.'

'I fear for her, Gengi.'

'Fear for you first! I know how you heal, so I don't need to hold back.'

He launches himself forward, too fast for a man of his size, swinging his mighty hammer towards my skull. I barely dodge underneath it, and before I have the chance to catch my breath, another swing flies towards me. I push the wind out from my hands, shoving myself backwards from his fierce strike.

He gives chase, lifting his weapon and charging forward. I steady myself in a defensive stance, and as the hammer comes down, I sidestep, shallowly cutting the giant man's arm. With no hesitation, his hammer smashes into my side, throwing me off my feet. I have never been hit so hard in my life. My arm throbs with pain, and he doesn't let up. His attacks keep coming in an endless wave. Even with my powers, I struggle to keep away from such a flurry. This man is a true champion master of war. I can't kill him. I don't want to kill him. Absorbing the sun as I retreat, my arm returns to normal, its strength fully restored. I have the unfair advantage, and yet, his energy seems that of a bottomless pit — my turn. I flash forward, just fast enough to catch Gengi off-guard, releasing the power of the sun. I use the winds to drive me up and over him in a flip, stabbing out with my blade and catching him on the neck – not deep enough to cause any real damage, but enough to make him bleed.

Before I have the chance for a secondary attack, he lurches back and simultaneously curves his hammer at me, forcing me to lift my blade to block the strike. His hammer smashes into my sword, shattering the blade into a thousand shards. I throw the last hilt at the Viking and move back. He stops attacking me.

'You might need another weapon, Youngling,' he smiles. If he wanted to win, I have no doubt he could beat me at any time. Even with my enhanced powers, he seems to be able to keep up with me.

It is not until now that I hear the crowds chanting for my death. The bloodlust in their stands seeping over us. If they felt shame earlier, then it has gone. Lost in combat like the lives of so many they have watched die on these sands. Sons and daughters, fathers and mothers, all for what?

I see a dagger on the floor, almost invisible it is so covered in sand.

'It's time, Jacob,' Gengi says, smiling at me and nodding his head, accepting his fate.

'There must be another way,' I shout. I don't want to kill this man.

'Do it, Jacob, do it now and be free. Claim your sword, avenge your father and live!'

I absorb the sun, stepping onward towards my friend, my foe, sliding underneath his hammer. I ask the breeze to halt me and lift me as I leap into the air behind Gengi. My arm wraps around his throat, dagger following, driving it toward his gullet to give him a swift death. I feel my tears pouring out of my eyes, another great man gone for nothing, but a voice makes me falter and halt my attack.

'*Jacob.*' I hear a whisper on the wind. It is the voice of Yerkasha. I look up to the battlements where she stands, a fierce gaze on her beautiful face. She lifts something in the air, a blade? My blade! *Meiyo.* She throws it over the edge of the area, and I release my friend from my grasp, absorbing the sun to make me shift too fast, the crowd gasping in awe of what they have just seen. I catch Meiyo in midair, feeling it's perfectly balanced craftsmanship, it's complex, folded steel blade, a picture of hope to me.

'Escape, Jacob, be free!' she shouts to me.

This changes everything.

'You should have finished me, Youngling.'

'No, my big friend, now we leave.'

The battlement doors burst open, a platoon of guards surround the exits.

'I hope you still have some energy left in that giant's body of yours, I say to my friend.

'You should ask your mother; she knows all about my energy.'

Always a moment of jest for Gengi. I kneel for a moment, placing my blade in front of me as an offering to the gods. I close down my eyes and absorb the sun. I feel my entire body come to life — the massive power curling up inside me. As I open my eyes, I notice that the very ground I am sat upon is scorched. Burnt from the suns glare. Even the great Gengi looks frozen in awe.

'Are you okay, Youngling?'

'I am better than okay.'

The sunlight fires me forward faster than any human can see. I zip past ten guards, disarming each one and striking them down with non-fatal blows.

'Come, let us leave this place.' I smile at my Viking friend.

Gengi hurries after me and through the hallways. We race down the corridor and hallway, searching for a route out of this labyrinth. I can hear guards in their hundreds chasing down the halls to stop us. I think about Yerkasha for a moment; what is happening to her? She will be in danger. I must save her.

We reach a set of enormous oak doors; they are locked and barricaded.

'This must be the way out.' Gengi shouts.

'Aye, step back, please.' I ask, curling the breeze around my wrists then arms, building a blast strong enough to rip the doors from their hinges.

Gengi holds up his hand, 'Do you hear that?'

I press my ear to the doors. Fighting? Who is fighting? The noise from the other side of the doors suddenly stops, and everything falls into silence. The footsteps of the arena guards, however, are growing nearer.

The door barricade is being released, and I hear the oak creaking and breaking.

'Move back, Gengi!' But before we get the chance, the doors split. Wood splinters around us, temporarily blinding us both.

As my vision returns, a delicate figure stands in front of us, and beside it, a man that is the size of a doorway wielding a bow and a patchwork cloak of greens and browns.

'Bipin... mother!'

'Hello, Jacob,' she says, giving her soft smile and comforting touch as I race over to her and her embrace.

'What are you doing here?'

'Bipin told me of your plight, and I want to help you.'

'This is your mother?' Exclaims Gengi. She is too beautiful to be your mother. You must look like your father, hey.'

Ignoring Gengi's flirtation with my mother, I look to Bipin, 'Does this not count as interfering?'

'It does not... I think.'

'We must escape. The shadow is upon us, and I don't think that we can defeat an entire army.'

'We must find Yerkasha first. I won't let her die because of me.'

'There is no time, son. If they catch you, they will kill you, and then all will be lost.'

The guards burst into the corridor. Not guards I have seen before. These guards are dressed in black, a sigil of angel wings cresting their shields, faces painted white.

'Kill the Nephilim,' their leader orders.

Kill the Nephilim. The words make me panic; how do they know what I am?

My mother whisps the winds around her wrists, letting out a mighty blast of energy into the guards. They topple back like twisted trees felled in a storm.

'Go! I will double back and find your Yerkasha.' Says Bipin.

'Don't let her die.'

'I will do all I can, Jacob, I promise.' And with that, he watcher rushes off down a different corridor.

We run as fast as we can without leaving the Viking behind. We make quick work of any soldiers in our path and reach the upper tiers. I glance over the battlements and see her, my love, Yerkasha. She is being dragged away by five guards, all wearing the same crest of angel wings. To the left, I see Ajax. He has a face of thunder, arms on his hips. Are they his soldiers? From the shadows, Bipin suddenly appears, bow in hand. How will he stop them? He cannot cause harm to any humans, that would mean interfering, and he would cease to be a watcher?

Bipin lifts his bow and pulls an arrow from its quiver. What is he doing! He releases it, striking the back of a guard who drops to the floor, dead. Four more arrows fly with perfect accuracy, and soon Yerkasha is stood all alone but for Ajax. Bipin looks at us, and for the first time since we met, I see him smile. *'I do this for you and the fate of the world, Nephilim. Don't waste it.'* A whisper on the wind says.

Ajax rushes over to Yerkasha, but Bipin does not strike him down. Instead, he joins them, and I see the white-suited man hurrying them through what looks like a secret door placed in the wall and out of sight.

'It is done, son. Lets us make haste.'

We rush out of the battlements and into the city grounds, dispersing with the frantic crowds. We go to my familiar alley and decide it is safer to wait there till nightfall — the entire city a buzz of what just happened — angry cries from people who have lost coin, and guards rushing around trying to keep the peace.

'What now?' I ask my mother

'Now we get back, *Senso*.'

Part 3

Chapter 28 – Even the Tiny Can Make a Difference

We leap the walls as night falls, both my mother and I holding an arm each as we wrap the winds around us and jump, holding a frightened Gengi. Dropping down as gently as we can, we enter the shantytown section of the city. It's darkness helping us to drift from shadow to shadow, avoiding all of the searching guards, who are scouring the city both inside and out.

We drift into narrow corridors avoiding both soldiers and those who live here. Gengi isn't the smallest of men, so trying to stay obscured is challenging.

'I will press forward, follow my lead,' I say to the others in a whisper.

I sneak to the edge of one of the buildings, peeking into the street covered in torchlight. The usual fires have been lit, the quiet dishevelled groups of residents sit around it with a painted picture of hopelessness brought on by the constant battle of hunger and hardship on their faces. I have no doubt they would give us up for the promise of coin or entrance into the grand city. Out of the shadows opposite, a troop of the dark clothing clad soldiers appear. They knock on doors and force their way into homes, all in the hope of finding us. I feel bad for these people. Their fear has been multiplied because of I – these evil warriors causing panic while families are disturbed and homes wrecked.

'I can't stand this. You two head back into the shadows above. I need to help these people.'

'Don't do anything stupid, Youngling,' the big man warns.

'I won't. Now be gone, get back into the shadows and wait for me. I will be fine.'

They both zip back down the narrow streets of the shantytown and disappear. I wrap the wind around my wrists and peek once again into the opening. One of the soldiers is dragging a man out of his shack by the throat. Why would they treat innocents like this? I won't have it. I blast the soldier from the shadows, the strike knocking him a good ten feet backwards, and he hits the floor with a great thud. The man rushes back into his home, slamming the door behind him. The soldier tries to get up but is left groaning on the floor in pain. I must be careful with that, I have grown stronger since my time training with the gladiators, and it would seem so have my powers, despite my not using them much.

The rest of the soldiers rush over to their fallen friend. He manages to point in my direction, or at least towards the darkness where I am hiding. That's enough for me, though. I poke my head out and wave to them. Exactly as I had hoped, they give chase. I fly through the narrowed alleyways, jumping from shadow to shadow, trying to lose them. The soldiers are adept, and these aren't just some imbecile city guards. These have been trained to deal with people such as me, but for what purpose?

I race as fast as I can and calling on a helpful breeze to drive me forwards. I seem to start losing them. I need to try and find the others, ensure their safety, and hopefully, they have managed to steer clear from these dark soldiers. I turn left into a street littered with old broken shacks. This place looks too low for anyone to live anymore, but the mass of shadow it is creating will help me go undetected. I leap into one of the buildings, its darkness enveloping me, and catch my breath for a moment, waiting to hear them pass.

The footsteps stop right outside. I hold my breath, hoping that they will pass me by. I take a quick peek through a hole in the wall, seeing the soldiers all standing to attention. A man walks through them, each giving him a salute as he passes.

'He is here somewhere. Find him, and you shall be rewarded greatly. Bring me the head of the Samurai,' I don't know this man, but his powerful voice and stature worry me. He is different, somehow. I can normally sense a human, their steps making noise in the wind, their breath giving them away, but nothing comes from this man.

'Yes, Onoskelis,' the soldiers say in unison.

Onoskelis, I have not heard of him, yet the name feels familiar? The soldiers start to search the area, each one with a silvered blade in hand. A loud explosion on one of the city walls draws them away. They rush off to investigate, and Onoskelis follows.

I wait for a moment or two and leave the house, rushing back to where I had left the others. Sneaking from shadow to shadow, I hear a whisper on the wind. '*Jacob, this way.*' It sounds like my mother, and so I rush off in the direction of the voice. I never realised how adept she is at manipulating the elements around her or how carefully my father had to restrain his power when we sparred. I wish I could have had more time with him, but I still have my mother, and I must focus on keeping her safe. I tiptoe around the clutter of homes, taking every step carefully, checking roofs, doorways and alleys to ensure I have not been followed. Whatever that explosion was, it has drawn the attention away from me and probably saved my life. Out of the shadows, a hand grabs my shirt and hurls me into a doorway. I grab at my sword only to find my Viking friend with a finger to his lips, gesturing me to follow.

'There are still guards all over, but we have found a place to hold up for the night,' he whispers.

'Where is my mother?'

'Did you hear that explosion?'

'Everyone did!'

'Well, that was her. I have no idea how she did it, but very winds around her swirled into a small tornado, only with the ferocity of a dragon's breath.

She blasted at a wall, caving in a large section. I know you have great power, but that is crazy. You could have crushed me in the arena.'

'You gave me more trouble than anyone I have ever fought, my friend, and you were trying to lose!'

'You are a good man, Jacob. Now follow me.'

We sneak off to a house on the bottom level of a stack of buildings. They look like a small gust of wind would bring the whole place down on us, yet they are robust, sturdy and on five floors. If they were going to fall, I am sure they would done so already.

As we enter the home, it is filled with the warm glow of a fire. I see my mother chatting with a small family.

'Jacob! Thank the gods. You are okay.'

'All thanks to you.'

She bows graciously. 'I was a warrior before a mother, but if anything, being a mother has made me more fierce,' she chuckles to herself, and I see something I thought was lost: her power, her smile, and herself.

'I'm happy to have you with me, mother.'

'This is Bretta, Fiok and little Hamsal,' my mother points to the family who are crowding the fire to keep warm.

'My thanks for letting us hide in your home, friends.'

'Both the parents bow to me, yet the little boy just stares. Not at me, but Gengi.'

'Hello, little one,' says Gengi, reaching out to shake the boy's hand. He clasps his giant hand around the tiny one of the boy and gives his usual big smile. The boy just stares, smiling back broadly.

'Apologies, champion, he is a big fan of yours.' Says the boys' mother, Bretta.

'Well, of course he is,' says Gengi. If any other person had said that, it would have been seen as arrogant, but Gengi has an aura of goodness about him. No wonder the man holds such adoration.

'Come, have a seat, you have had a stressful time of it, and you are probably hungry,' Fiok gestures for us to take a seat near the fire. This house is much more than it seemed from the outside. The main room is more significant than expected, it has two doorways which probably lead to separate bedrooms, but I was expecting it to be just one tiny room. It is far better cared for than I could have imagined. It is clean, has a warm fire, which seems to heat the place well, and a few books.

'May I please ask you a question about this place?' I ask Bretta.

'You can, Samurai.'

'Please, it's Jacob.'

She nods and smiles at me.

'Why do you live here? Why choose a place like this?'

'The promise of a better life. We travelled here from the deep south, hoping to make a fortune and get Hamsal schooled. This is the only place that offers such things.'

'And has that happened?'

'No. It is not the place we believed it to be. Firstly, you have to pay one thousand coins just to get into the city. Once in, you will have to pay double that for a home. We figured we could save that amount and eventually get ourselves in, but the soldiers charge high taxes for us to stay here.

Protection money, they say. We barely have enough to purchase food and water.'

'Purchase food and water?' I ask. 'There is a river less than two miles from here. It is fresh running water and is bursting at the banks with fat fish. Why do you not take a walk up there?'

Bretta looks to the floor, her husband holding her on the shoulder, comforting her. 'We are not permitted to do that. You need a license to collect water and fish, and that license costs a lot of gold. Not only that, but it must then be sold to the city and a percentage given to the tower,' Fiok responds.

'You must pay a tithe for water… they do not own the river, the rivers and land belong to us all,' I say.

'Some have tried to fish under cover of darkness, but they all meet the same fate. Hands chopped from the wrists and branded as thieves.' The father starts to cry, hugging his wife tight. 'I brought us here, and now we cannot leave. They control everything.'

It all suddenly makes sense. None of the people here spoke to me when I first entered the city.

They all looked frightened, and they have all lost hope. This city is a virus on these poor people. I wish I could do something to help them.

'I wish I could give you all the gold I had won, my friends,' Says Gengi, a tear slowly making a path down his cheek. I had no idea this was going on out here. One day I will return, pick up my winnings and spread it to you all. No one should live like this.'

'It is my doing,' Fiok says. 'I brought us here, and it is my fault we live like this. We once had a farm with pigs and sheep. We lived well, but greed got the better of me.'

'No, Fiok. This is not your fault. This is the fault of the city and those who rule it.' My anger starting to show as I raise my voice.

'Once this is over, I shall return and make these people pay, I vow it. A Vikings fury is not to be trifled with, and nor is his promise.' The big man stands and bows to the family. The young boy cheers him and gets back to staring.

A knock on the door makes me jump. I unsheath my sword and see Gengi and my mother followed suit.

'Quick, hide here,' the young boy pushes aside a piece of wall, opening up a small hidden cavern in the back of the house. 'We use it to hide when the soldiers come.'

We prise ourselves into the hole. It barely fits us, but we just about manage it.

'Open the door by order of Neodias.'

I have a terrible realisation that we have left the family out there, vulnerable and alone.

'If the guards get violent, we get rid of them as quickly and quietly as possible. I will not let this family be harmed.' Both Gengi and my mother agree with a silent nod of their heads.

'Why did you take so long to open your door, scum? What are you hiding?'

'Nothing, friends. We were just about to sit and eat. Would you care to join us?' Says Bretta.

'You want to kill us with that gruel, do you?' The soldiers laugh.

I can hear them searching around the space. Shifting and throwing various furniture out of the way and rummaging into the bedrooms.

'Wow, you are a real soldier!' I hear young Hamsal say. 'Can I touch your sword, please, just quickly?'

'No, boy. This is sharp, you will hurt yourself. We can't have anyone getting hurt now, can we?'

The soldier sounds snide and evil. If he touches a single hair on any of their heads, it will be the last thing he does.

'Oh, please, you are all so brave. I want to be a warrior just like you someday.'

'Listen, boy. Step away, we have a job to do, and you are getting in my way and testing my patience.'

'Come on, Smit, he is just a boy. He is admiring you, which is more than your mother does,' says another voice.

The other soldiers laugh. Jibing him, encouraging him to allow the boy a peek.

'Okay, okay. Here.' I hear the sword being partially unsheathed and automatically ready my blade.

'Oh my! It is sharp. You must be able to kill so many bad people with this.'

'That's right, boy. I have gutted many a villain with this blade. I treat it like I would treat my wife.'

'If you could get one, you ugly bastard.' The same voice as before laughs, and once again, the rest of the guards chuckle in unison.

'Arg, enough of this. There is nothing here but awful gruel and a stench of death. Let's not linger; we have a reward to fetch!'

The soldiers leave as swiftly as they had entered. We wait for a few moments, and the Hamsal pushes the false wall away.

'You are safe now,' he says, beaming at Gengi.

'You are the bravest man I have ever met,' the Viking says to the boy, who, in return, looks like he has just become a champion himself. 'See, Hamsal. Even the tiny can make a difference, don't ever lose hope, and always be brave and true.'

Chapter 29 - Like the Winds

The night leaves us — no more disturbances or visits from the unwanted soldiers. The morning brings with it a beautiful golden sunrise and a feeling of hope. We are still not away from the city, but the noises of clattering weapons and armour have drifted away. The calm of bird song and a slight breeze bring with it whispers. People up at the break of dawn, still talking about last nights chaos. This morning we must make a break for it. I feel terrible for leaving this family behind, but where we are going is far more dangerous than the evils on the city's outskirts.

The rest of the group stir and Bretta has already started preparing breakfast.

'You must eat before you leave, friends.'

'I can never thank you and your family enough for what you have done.' I say, taking the sweet porridge from her. It smells so good, and I am sure this would normally be a treat for them, yet they share it with us willingly. We are strangers to them, yet they do all they can to help us in our time of greatest hour of need. They deserve a better life than this.

'We can not thank you enough, Jacob. You have given us far more than shelter. You have given us hope.' Bretta takes my hand in her own. 'Don't forget us, okay?'

'I shall not. I vow it.'

My mother leaves before us, off to grab a horse for Gengi, else he slows us down. No one has seen her, so she can come and go as she pleases, which is handy when you are in hiding. Gengi and the boy sit playing games of slap fist, and he lets the boy win. Fiok stands by the fire, watching the flames dance.

'Such things have always enchanted me,' he says. 'The way the flames look like they are dancing on the wood, yet causing the wood to ruin. It is a strange thing, knowing that the death of one thing brings about life to others. When does that stop?'

I stand and walk to him. 'I wish I had all the answers, my friend,' I respond.

'I think you are this fire. Not just you, Jacob, but Telaá and Gengi too. I think you are the fire that will bring death to those that deserve it and that you will bring us warmth and security.'

'I will do all I can to make that happen, and so will the others.'

'I believe you, I really do.'

My mother enters the house, nodding that it is time to leave.

'We must leave you now. Thank you once again for all you have done.'

Gengi hands the boy a pendant carved from wood in the evening past.

'It is the hammer of a Viking god called Thor,' he says to the boy. 'It will keep you brave and help him to grow into a powerful warrior that will protect the innocent.'

The boys' smile stretches as far as the oceans reach, and his eyes shine with pure joy. 'I will treasure it always Gengi, king of the world.'

'It is a small token for your brave actions on the night passed. Keep it close, and be a good boy for your parents.'

Little Hamsal's cheeks flush, and tears fill his eyes. He grasps the giant in a warm embrace, one that causes Gengi to beam from ear to ear. He would make a great father.

We leave the house quickly and as silently as possible, covering ourselves with old blankets and wearing them as shawls, trying to disguise our appearance. Gengi is the most difficult to keep inconspicuous, simply because of his stature. We drift out of the house and start moving among the crowds. There is still quite a buzz around after yesterdays happenings. So we try and mingle with the crowd, hoping that we are mistaken for another family of traders, getting on with our days business.

We meander away from the ramshackle town outside the wall; all three of us seem to take a deep sigh as we pull further away from danger and those terrible dark soldiers.

'You three!' I hear a shout from a distance. 'Halt!'

I look back, seeing three of the regular soldiers approaching.

'No one is to leave without a permit today. Sorry for the inconvenience, but it is by order of the City.'

My mother looks at me, 'No harm, they are innocents.'

'As you wish,' I respond. I collect the breeze around me, being careful not to blast them too hard. I turn and fire. My wrists and hands explode in a storm of high winds, knocking the three off their feet and pushing them back some ten meters.

'Time to go,' Says the Viking, who launches himself onto the stolen horse.

My mother and I take a moment to absorb the sun, unleashing it and start to run alongside the galloping horse. Gengi looks at us, shaking his head in amazement.

'What's wrong big man? Never seen a person outrun a horse?'

'No, Jacob, I haven't. But I am looking at someone who has the face of one.' Gengi laughs to himself hysterically, and we run, fast and far, away from the danger and back to the quest at hand, find the Senso blade, and get revenge.

Chapter 30 – The Chase and the Choice

We head out toward the snowy mountains. It looms ahead like a giant white wraith, the snow blowing off the tip in swaths, giving the illusion of a single white wing expanding from its peak. Within it, the Archivist, the Senso blade, and my revenge. We keep racing forward, the horse managing to keep up for the most of it and only occasionally having to stop for food and water.

Behind us, the army of dark soldiers gives chase. It contrasts the snow peaks in front like a dark shadow, following us everywhere we go. I can't believe they would send so many men after we three. Why?

I wonder what has become of Yerkasha, Bipin and Ajax? Did they escape? Are they alive? I wish I could return to them right now to ensure their safety and hold that beautiful woman in my arms again. I have thrown her into this mess, along with my mother and friend Gengi.

'This is my fight. I do not want you to put yourselves in danger for this.' I say.

'No offence, Youngling, but I have been putting myself in danger since well before I met you. I am also not ready to retire to the river yet, and I haven't even found my buxom wife to be. So if it is okay with you, I shall remain,' the big man bows, his usual quirky smile spreads across his face.

'You are also stuck with me, Son. This is a fight your father and I should have been a part of, so it is about time I fulfilled what I am supposed to do.'

'I don't understand, Mother?'

'The summoning, Jacob. You remember when Bipin first came to us?' she explains. 'We are Nephilim, the sons and daughters of the angels of heaven. We were born to protect and teach the human race. Some two thousand years ago, the last great war saw the almost complete annihilation of the human race. The corruption and greed overtook compassion and common sense, causing them to hate each other. Borders were made, alienating them from each other, technology surpassed wisdom, and the planet itself began to die. Each wanted what the other had and were willing to kill for it. Overwhelmed with ego, they fought with weapons of destruction you would never imagine. Flying machines holding explosive devices, armoured land machines and weapons that could kill a man from miles away. That brought about the ruin and near-complete destruction of man. They became disconnected from the Earth, ruining it for a very long time. Nature almost gave up. We were told to keep watch of man as they grew back into themselves.'

She continues her explanation, telling me about the shadow that looms over us. The feeling of corruption and greed overwhelmed her. She felt it in the city of Neodias more than she had before or at any place or time. The shadow was so close then that the burden almost crushed her spirit like a great weight was placed on her shoulders.

I am surprised to find out that my father had been the leader of the Nephilim but chose to leave when my mother and he fell in love. He was gifted the Senso blade as a conduit to defeat the shadow should it appear again. The blade itself can absorb the powers of all seven Nephilim, unleashing it in a fury of light upon the corruption. It can only be defeated in that way, whatever this shadow is?

Is the Archivist this shadow?

Is he to blame for all of the pain and suffering in the city?

'Look there, Jacob.' Gengi points into the distant shadow army. 'A small group of them have peeled away in front and are gaining.'

'Then let us not linger. We make for the mountain through the plains, and we can hopefully lose them in the snow.'

The poor horse looks uncomfortable at having to carry such a huge man on its back at speed, but it is a warrior, and like he, it presses on.

As fast as we manage to run, they manage to gain. As they draw closer, we can see that the small band contains only four men riding giant silver horses. Each has gleaming armour of silvers and blacks, with a white helm shaped like a skull.

'There are only four! We can finish them easily with you two and your magical powers.' Gengi scoffs.

'We must press on. If the rest of the army catches up while we are fighting, then it would be

over. Four we can take, but four-hundred, we cannot,'
I say. Gengi looks disappointed, but I fear he just
wants to see us use our powers again. 'Don't worry.
Your time will come, Viking. And when it does, you
will be as fierce as you were in the arena.'

He puffs his chest out a little at that, making
himself larger and more heroic-looking, but with a
smile the size that matches his stature. For a man that
has seen so much death, he is so positive.

The plains start to disappear. A gentle fall of
snow begins to surround us. It blankets the floor,
working its way into patches to hiding the greenness
of the grass below. Its icy touch falls on my cheeks as
I race forward, far too fast for a man.

'We must slow here, Jacob. The snow will not
be our friend if we flash move. Our feet can get
unsteady and cause — problems,' my mother states.

I bow to her wisdom, slowing the pace down
to a regular run. It takes me back to before I had my
awakening, all those miles my father made me run.
The peace and calm of it all, watching the world pass
by me, the meadows a flutter with creatures that dwell

there, and the mud. I cannot forget the mud. I haven't seen the snow close up before. Nor felt it on my skin. It calls to me much as the rain does. I feel it is a part of me as the other elements.

'Mother, can we control the snow?'

'Yes, we can. Just remember not to control it and the wind together. It can be disastrous, as you know,' she gives me a wink, collecting the snow as it falls in her hand, till a small ball of white takes shape. 'See, as it is more solid than rain, you can gather it together. Once it is gathered, then you can use the other elements to help.' She takes a deep inhalation, this time calling to the winds as she blows the ball of snow away. It launches from her hand as speed, splatting into the back of Gengi's head.

'Do you mind…I am already cold,' he laughs.

While we run, I practice. Gathering the snow into balls as it falls from the heavens. I fire them off in different directions. It is actually quite fun. Who would have thought throwing a ball of snow could be a game?

For a short moment, we forget the chase. We run, we play, we laugh. For the first time in a long time, I see my mother looking happy. She is far stronger than I had imagined, and I feel a pang of guilt that I had underestimated how strong and powerful she is. After all, a Nephilim, like my father and me. Her prowess and fluidity are just as substantial as my father, and what she lacks in the sheer strength my father had, she more than makes up for by her fantastic agility and speed. She is as quick and nimble as a prowling cat.

As snow grows thicker, our pace has slows considerably, but we trundle on. Even Gengi's horse is struggling to force its way through the blanket of white. My mother and I have absorbed the sun to keep us warm, but I fear how much of this Gengi can take. We have only the gladiator garb and what blankets we stole to keep him warm. He shows no discomfort though, pushing forward and urging his horse on.

'I fear that the great army that follows can trample this snow covering in moments, allowing them to catch us up,' my mother claims.

Gengi looks to us both, his usual grin infested face, dark and serious, 'You must leave me behind. Go complete your mission.'

'Gengi, I wish you would stop being so dramatic. You have already offered your life once, and this makes me think you don't want to live at all. We are not leaving your side, my friend.'   I respond lightheartedly.

'Ha! I just want for a heroic death, so that maybe a woman or three will sing my name after I reach the top of the world tree and my heavens.'

'You probably have children all over Neodias, Gengi. I doubt they will be singing, more cursing your name for leaving a babe to every woman's belly that you've come across.'

'I think you are right, Youngling. Maybe I should die in the snow, then to the moaning cries of those women.'

'Do you hear that?' My mother asks. The neighing of distant horses and clattering of armour and weapons on the wind. 'They are gaining!'

'I hear nothing?' The Viking says, clearly bemused at our being able to hear anything but the crushing of snow and the breeze in the pines surrounding us.

'The winds do warn us. If the army is gaining at such speed, where are the four horsemen we saw?' I ask, drawing my sword.

Through the trees, four beautiful silver horses emerge, as quiet as a whisper. For the first time, we see the giants atop them. Their armour is glinting as if fresh from the smithy. The skulls on their helms, making it seem like the dead themselves, have appeared to stop us. My mother bursts into action, not waiting to see what they do. She leaps at the first, blade forward in a perfect attack. The first of the warriors leaps up to meet her, his jump is a little too high for a human and meeting her sword with his own and making her crash back into the snow.

'These demons can fight!' Shouts Gengi, letting his horse go and pulling his hammer from across his back. He rushes forward as fast as his human legs can, swinging for another. The demon's horse rises onto its hind legs, making it twice the size of my large friend, who ducks underneath it and slams at the thigh of the second warrior. Gengi misses, but the soldier's foot does not, kicking him in the face and knocking the Viking off his feet and into a stumble. Gengi rises, unphased by the strike, and charges forward again. The horseman dismounts and unsheathes his own weapon, a curved blade scimitar, none like I have seen before. Its blade is red as if permanently stained by blood.

'Kill the Nephilim,' a booming voice says. I cannot tell if it was from one or all of the men in front of us.

'We must not linger here. The army is close. Mother, grab Gengi,' I shout.

She leaps over the big man, who is locked in combat with one of the deathly four, blasting his opponent with a storm like wind and leaving him flat on his back at least fifteen meters away. She grabs Gengi by the arm, and I race over to join them, taking hold of Gengi's' other.

'Together, mother, ready?'

'Ready!'

We both swirl the wind around our bodies, leaping an impossible distance away, then curling the wind underneath us to slow our fall. In the distance, we see the demons getting back on their horses. We absorb what sun we can, keeping hold of Gengi and flashing forward at great speed, yet not our maximum as it would probably tear poor Gengi apart, just enough to gain some distance away from the four who are chasing.

'I feel sick,' Gengi says.

'Sorry, Gengi, it is necessary to get us to safety. They are not normal men we fight,' my mother explains.

'Please don't jump like that again. I am a man, not a bird. My big body is not made for flying, Youngling.'

Chapter 31 – Corruption

Using our combined powers, we manage to escape the four, trudging our way through the thick snows, listening to the winds as they give away our pursuers position. We make our way deeper to the pine forest – there, we will have considerably more cover. The woods will slow our pace even more, but it is a sacrifice we must make. The plains are growing colder each step we take, and I am fearful that Gengi, despite his protests, will freeze to death. I wish that I could transfer some of my solar power to him. The forest will provide some cover and some respite from the chilling winds. We move as silently as we possibly can, covering our tracks using the power of the breeze. It is strenuous work. With the sunlight shaded by the snow, the continued use of our abilities has started to take its toll on both my mother and me.

As soon as we enter, the temperature seems to improve. It is slight but will hopefully stop the giant Viking from shaking so much.

'We need food and shelter before the night comes,' says my Mother.

Gengi's eyes light up. 'Agreed, especially on the food part.'

'Okay, there is a river I can hear close by. It is not yet frozen, so it will still draw animals close. Be as silent as possible. With more humans this close by, they will be twitchy and will easily fear and flee.' I unsheath my sword and shift as quietly as possible toward the flowing river.

Gengi is surprisingly agile for such a big man. His feet plant on the floor with almost no noise. My mother and I use the winds to glide over the frozen ground, making barely a mark on the carpet of snow. As we get closer, the ground turns from beautiful white to brown, coated in a foul black sludge. Something is polluting the river. The smell then hits us. A mix of death and oil drifts over with a gust of breeze. Before long, we come across the river, now running with nothing that resembles water.

'Don't get close, look!' I point to the banks. A cluster of dead wolves lay close to its banks. They had attempted to drink from the river, it would seem, and it killed them all. Everywhere we look, we see that entwined with the sludge and snow are more corpses. Animals are rotting, their flesh turning green as the pollution takes over.

Gengi glances around, his face paling with the smell and sight of it. 'This is so sad. These beautiful creatures all dead because of this. The river probably runs to the bottom of the mountain. Odin only knows how much death it has caused.'

'I agree, my friend. We must find its source, although you do understand that the city of Neodias was similar. Do you not?'

'I never got to see much of the city. That was reserved for our lady's favourite.'

'I'm sorry, Gengi. We will find out what causes this, and we will destroy it, I promise.'

The Viking nods to me in agreement. His face, for the first time, looks angry.

'These wolves are freshly dead. So if you both do not mind, I will make use of what I can.' Gengi strides over to the dead pack and gently strokes their beautiful white pelts.

'I wouldn't risk eating them.' I say

'I do not intend to eat these beautiful creatures. Just borrow their coats, so I do not become carrion for the sludge.'

He carefully rids four wolves of their fur, fastening them together skillfully and wiping them down in the clear snow further in the wood. Once he is done, we make our way up the river in the hope of finding the source er-route to the home of the Archivist. If he is responsible for this corruption of the land, then there is even more reason to stop him. How can people be so indifferent to the damage they are causing to the land. I can see why humans in the past couldn't be trusted to act of their own accord; it's like they would burn the very home they live in just to stay warm.

The army grows ever closer, and as the night draws in, we are forced to make a shelter. We pull the snow down, using it to create a small cavern for us to hide. Gengi watches, his big smile returning as we meld the snow as it falls, directing it into curved walls that lead to a shallow roof to stop more snow blowing in. Where the walls meet the roof, we carve small holes to allow the smoke from the fire to disperse evenly and spread the smoke so that it would hopefully be invisible to the naked eye. We collect wood and create a bed for Gengi. He protests that the lady should get to rest first and foremost. We explain that we require a lot less sleep if we have absorbed the suns power. Eventually, he believes us and starts to snooze by the fire.

In the darkness, the noise of the army grows closer. We are off the main path, so we shouldn't be seen, but I fear that the speed they are travelling will mean that they will easily pass us by before the sun decides to rise. The four horsemen no doubt lurching around, searching for the three of us. What are they, I wonder? They were like giants with too much speed and strength for a human. Yet, I could say the same for Gengi. When we fought, he was like a Nephilim himself. So much power for a regular man. And what of Yerkasha and Bipin? Are they safe? Why did Ajax help them?

My mother breaks my thoughts by whispering to me, 'Is he a human, Jacob?' pointing at Gengi.

'I think so? He is a very skilled human, but a human nonetheless, I believe.'

'I am not referring to his skill, although you are right. I am referring to his demeanour. He is strong yet gentle. He is skilled yet humble. These are rare among humans.'

'Maybe he was made for more than just this life, mother?'

'I like him. He is an honourable man. Let's make sure he stays alive. The world needs more like him upon it.' She smiles in only the way my mother can. She has come to life on this quest, and I am glad I can share it with her.

The morning comes with the sound of birdsong. The night held very little in action, but my mother did hunt successfully, getting us some food for breakfast, to the glee of Gengi especially. We make our way out of the shelter and back up the river. Gengi looks even bigger, adorning those four wolf pelts. He could be a king if I didn't know him any better. There is no sign of the army until the path and the river meet. We see the trampled snow all over the route. The army has clearly been and gone, heading towards the Archivist's home. As we get to a somewhat higher point, we see it. The enormous black complex, staring out at us. It deeply contrasts the brilliant whites of the mountains' edge, like a dark cancerous wort on pale silky skin. At the bottom of the wall, a dark liquid froths out of its bowels into the river, the same sludge from below, eating away at the pure ground and water it falls upon. Smoke billows out from beyond the walls, undoubtedly causing the same damage to the sky as it does the earth. This place is hideous, and I can feel it surrounded by death.

As we sneak closer to the walls, we can see they are made from blackened steel. They are nowhere near as tall as the walls of Neodias, but I fear that there is a far more powerful army within them. A constant heavy thrumming of noise comes from beyond the steel, loud banging and smashing of metal on metal.

'I'm going to check it out. Keep an eye on Gengi, Mother. I won't be long.'

I gather the breeze and leap up to the top of the wall, landing softly onto the edge. The walls are just a thin palisade, so no room for soldiers to roam up here. I balance myself and crouch to make myself small, hopefully evading the prying eyes that might be checking the fortress edge.

The whole area is alive with movement. Men and women covered in ash and dirt rush around, heaving huge pieces of metal from place to place. Soldiers watch over them, whips in their hands, to keep them *motivated* to work. They are constructing huge metal carts with what looks to be a projectile firing mechanism on their roof. What are these metallic beasts?

At the far end of the interior, I see the army again. At the forefront of them, the four horsemen sit on their silver horses as still as death. Then I see him. One man standing in front of them all. Could that be him? The Archivist?

'Winds, bring me his words,' I ask, hoping they will give me some notion of what is going on here.

'The tanks are almost done, and the guns have been tested and are ready.'

Tanks, guns?

'The Nephilim are on their way,' the four horsemen seem to say in unison. *'You must prepare,*

Archivist. They are more powerful than the others you have encountered.'

'Bah, you mock me. With all this firepower, what chance will they have? Just like their illustrious and rebellious leader, his head removed with a single shot before he even saw it coming. And the Senso blade, mine,'

So this is the Archivist! I feel my rage start to boil. Every part of me wants to flash over there and separate his head from its shoulders, justice being served. Yet, what good will it do? The army would destroy me in seconds. I cannot fight them all.

'The Senso blade does not belong to you, Archivist. It belongs to Onoskelis, the one true ruler. That is why we have been sent. Kill the Nephilim. Take back the sword. You have been careless to let them find you.'

'I should have realised this when he sent his cronies out.'

Onoskelis, I have heard that name before.

I gently float back down the wall to my mother and Gengi and explain what I had seen and heard.

'Onoskelis? Are you sure that is the name you heard?' My mother asks.

'Yes, why?'

'Onoskelis is a name I have heard of too, only through the ancient Nephilim teachings. He was paramount in the cause of the corruption of human hearts during the great war. Jacob, he was revealed as the angel of corruption. He is the one that we were supposed to put an end to using the *Senso* blade, which is why it is imperative that we retrieve it. He must also be the shadow that I can sense.'

'Well, why can't I sense him? I was hidden just feet away from him at Neodias?'

'I can't explain that I'm afraid, Son.'

'I simply have no idea what's going on.' Gengi says, breaking me out of my thoughts. 'But are we going to go in there and kill that man? My hammer is getting thirsty.'

I nod to the big man, 'I suggest we sneak in at night. I will steal away the *Senso* blade and kill the Archivist.'

'And what are we to do?' Both my mother and Gengi ask.

'We cannot take on an army.'

Gengi rubs his stomach and frowns. 'Have you not seen me when I am hungry?'

'Sorry, I will not risk your lives. We wait till dark, and I will go in alone.'

Chapter 32 – The Archivist

As the sun peacefully slips away, I make my way back from the tiny snow home we have made close by and silently move back to the fortress wall. There was very little sun for me to absorb during the day. The white blanket of cloud has covered most of the sky, leaving very little light. I will have to rely on the breeze to assist me, and hopefully, I won't get into any trouble that will require me to heal myself.

I leap onto the top of the wall, peering over to ensure no guards await my descent into the fortress. The noises and bustle of the ever working slaves cover my sound as I drop on the enemy side of the wall. Every part of me wants to help these poor people. The soldiers that guard them, wielding savage-looking whips, with knotted ends that would rend the flesh off your back like a hot knife through butter. Some of the slaves have already received its kiss. I can tell from the tears in their overshirts and stains of old blood on their backs. I will save you all, I promise.

I stealthy move between the shadows of the fires, steering away from both the eyes of slaves and soldiers alike. The desperate will do anything to be saved, and I have no idea how they would react to seeing a stranger moving amongst them. I head toward the building on the far west side of the courtyard, that is where I saw the Archivist disappear after speaking to the four horsemen.

The army still appears to be on high alert. They have been split into groups, patrolling the edges of the wall, armed and ready for battle. I do not see the four, however. Perhaps they have already left with *Senso* and are entrusting the Archivist to bring about my death. He managed to kill my father with these terrible weapons, but I can use this overconfidence to my advantage. I just have to make sure he doesn't see me till I want him to.

I linger for a moment, the shadows my temporary home. He must be here somewhere, and I can't just search every room in the complex without being caught sooner or later. I am not left waiting long. For the first time, I get a good look at the man that killed my father and sent me on this journey. I am surprised by his appearance. His white hair giving away his age, I expected a warrior, but he looks old and frail. Eye lenses are perched on his crooked nose, and his back is bent over a little too much. He saunters around the grounds, taking note of the work going on. He seems unphased by the horrific sights, approaching the slaves and saying things to them that I can't hear, although their eyes give away the fear he brings to them.

After his circuit and stopping to talk to some of the guards, who turn their attention to the slaves and start making use of their horrible whips. He walks back to the building where I hide. This is my chance. I follow him inside. Thankfully, it is not very well lit in here. I shift from shadow to shadow, the wind curling around my feet, making my tread as soft as a feathers when it strikes the ground. After a few moments, he turns left. I follow him into a smallish room covered floor to ceiling with diagrams of the monsters of metal being built outside. A large wooden desk sits in the middle, more plans strewn across it and a lot of paper, ink and quills.

He takes a seat at his desk and looks directly into the shadow where I am hiding.

'Will you take a seat, Jacob?' He says.

I step out of the corner and step into the light, unsheathing my blade and pointing it at the man I call my enemy. 'You killed my father, and now, I have come to kill you.'

'Yes, yes. A theatrical entrance, my boy.'

'You mock me? That is unwise for your last words.'

'My last words? I'm afraid that once again, you have underestimated humans. You Nephilim are all the same, pompous, arrogant, and all underestimate us.'

He knew I was there, he managed to kill my father without being seen, and he has been building machines that should have been lost to history. He is right. I have underestimated him.

'Still, I am here, and you are about to die.' I step forward, 'And that time is now!'

'I don't think it is, my boy. Yet, if you feel you must, then please do go ahead. I have lived for a long time, perhaps too long, but long enough to know that Onoskelis is the one to bring true paradise to a place tarnished by god.'

'Who is this Onoskelis?'

'He is the truth. He will bring the tyranny of the gods and Nephilim to an end.'

'We are here to protect humans and guide them.'

'I don't think you understand, you naive boy.' He shakes his head, rising from his desk and starts to shift through his books. 'Bear with me a moment if you would.'

I don't know why I hesitate, but something makes me hold back. Maybe it's the fact that he is showing not a single ounce of fear while staring death in the eyes.

'Ah, here we go.' He pulls a few books out of his shelf and makes his way back to his desk. 'These are all books of religion. We have the bible, Christian, of course. We have the Quaran, and we have the stories of the Vikings, who conquered the world. Among many others, actually. Do you know what these books are?'

'I do not.' I admit.

'These are the rules and stories that God put here for humans to follow. Two thousand years ago, these books caused the almost complete destruction of man. They are the biggest pile of hypocritical shit ever to adorn the pages of a book.'

'And what does this have to do with me?'

'You are a creature of God, my lad. You are a part of these stories. You are a part of that hypocrisy. You see, this god that everyone used to love, the one who created us all as an experiment, is evil.'

'I don't understand what this has to do with you killing my father?' I ask

'Your father was the man who was to bring an end to Onoskelis. Him and his *Senso* sword. I had to stop him. Humans must be left to their own devices, to be allowed to see how they live without the influences of any Gods.'

'You are wrong. We are here to help humans, not to influence them.'

'Your god, my boy, is evil.' He pulls out another book from the pile on his desk. 'Do you know what this is?' He throws me the book.

I catch the book in my free hand and read the title; it is a medical journal on various cancers. 'Yes, it is a list of ailments.'

'Correct. Now switch to page seventy-three.'

I do as he asks, rifling through the pages till I reach a page titled Cancer among Children.

'Did you know that there are over two hundred types of cancer that children can die from? Some of them more horrific than others, but all of them generally have the same effect, the end of the child's life. Are you telling me that you have a loving and kind god? He created us. He gave us these cancers. These are just one aspect of the horrible things out there created to make us suffer.'

'There must be an explanation for it. Perhaps he didn't create us. Perhaps we were found on this planet and required guidance to help us grow? If Onoskelis is telling the truth, then why does he require these metal machines of death? They will not stop the gods, just the humans that dare fight him. He wants to rule us.'

'Better the devil you know, Jacob.'

'No, I will stop him. But first, I will stop you.'
I point my sword at the old man.

He laughs, smiling a large evil grin toward me, his frailties washing away suddenly. 'You fool. I have your friends already. The four knew where you were hiding in your pathetic hideout. Your mother and Gengi are mine, and if I die, they die. The four have been created to feel the Nehpilim's presence and to search for and destroy them.'

He has tricked me, that vile old man. I have underestimated him once again. I mistook his so-called frailty as a weakness, and it stalled me.

'To hell with you old man!'

'We are already in hell, my boy. Now we will let Onoskelis show us an alternative.'

The four burst through the door of his little room and wrestle me to the ground, a little too powerful to be mere humans.

They drag me outside, to where my mother, Gengi and the army awaits. Both of them are bloody. They didn't go down without a fight.
'Are you both okay?' I ask.

'We are, but those four idiots can hit hard,' says Gengi. He laughs unsurprisingly, almost like he is happy to have finally met his match.

'Did you kill the Archivist, Jacob?' My mother asks.

'I'm sorry I have failed. Not only that, but I allowed you to get captured.'

'It is your turn to stop being dramatic, Youngling. It isn't over until the fat and buxom lady sings. Sings to me, that is.' The Viking laughs out loud, infuriating one of his guards who strikes him across the face. 'You hit like a small child, friend.'

'So, here are all the trouble makers together.' The Archivist says, making his way over to us with *Senso* in his hands. 'And to think of all the trouble you caused in Neodias, I mean honestly, their soldiers need some serious training. Although armed with my guns and tanks, no one will be able to cross them. The fate of humans will be in new hands, and with it, a time of peace will be here.'

'Peace through fear!' I shout defiantly.

'Peace nonetheless, Jacob. The time of the Nephilim will soon be over.'

The old man hands the sword to the leader of the four, who attaches the sheathed blade to his waist.

'We have the weapon, and we have the Nephilim. Well done, Archivist, Onoskelis will be pleased with your work here,' they say in unison. 'We take our leave and will return for the arms in three weeks. Make sure they are ready.'

'Tell his lordship; I look forward to seeing him.'

The old man walks back to his building. 'I will be right back.'

My mother, along with Gengi, are thrown into a clearing by the fortress wall.

'What will happen to them?' I ask the leader of the four.

'They will die. All Nephilim must die.'

'What about me?'

'You are something different. We cannot sense you, yet you have the powers of a Nephilim. We must take you to Onoskelis. He will decide what to do with you.'

'Can't you at least let Gengi go? He is no Nephilim.'

'He is an irrelevant trouble maker. We have no use for him.'

'Then you will let him go?'

'No. He holds no purpose, so he will also die.'

I can't let this happen. My mother and Gengi must survive. Yet we are just three, and a captured three at that. How will I stop them? I can't do this alone.

'Oh, wait a moment, please.' I hear the Archivist shout. 'Jacob…I want you to know that I could have killed you as easily as I killed your pathetic father. I was just told I must spare your life, a shame really. I would have liked to have seen you die, just like the rest of your family will. Let us start with your mother, shall we?' He holds up a large metal object. A long barrel protrudes from the end of it and some sort of viewing device on the top. 'Do you recognise this? Of course you don't. This is what killed your father, my boy. Seems fitting that it is what will end your mother and friend too.'

Chapter 33 – The Army of Three

No, this can't be happening. My mother looks at me, her smile still warm as she faces her death.

'Don't worry, Jacob. I leave to meet your father in the heavens. You must not let this consume you.'

'No, Mother! I cannot lose you both.' I scream, the tears starting to make their way down my cold cheeks.

I search around the courtyard, just hoping something will make this mad man stop. I can't lose my family and my only friend. Then I see it! The suns rise. The first light turning the sky into embers of power for me to absorb. It calls to me as a babe would call to its mother, like a river calls to the sea. But what else is this I feel? The coming of rain above me, grey clouds fill the sky, and I start to feel the first drops on my face. I know what I need to do!

I gather together the power of all three elements, the rain, the sun and the winds. My father warned that combining just two elements is explosive. What can I create by asking all three to dance?

'Let's get this done before the rain gets me soaked,' the Archivist complains as he lifts his eye the viewing device.

'No!' I shout, absorbing as much power as I can. 'This is your end, Archivist!'

'Someone shut him up. He is putting me off my aim.'

I feel the power surging through my veins. The elements start to dance around my body. The four horsemen approach. The rain begins falling hard, and the wind starts to swirl around my body, creating a torrent of power.

'Stop him NOW!' The Archivist shaking from the force of the wind, which wraps itself around my body. I unleash the sun, it combines with the other elements, and just as I suspected, the results are incredible. Fury in the form of lightning surges from out of my body in a massive explosion. The crackling of light, water and wind creating a perfect storm from my body, firing out in every direction. My limbs, chest and back release pure light. How am I still standing? How has the storm not destroyed me?

Suddenly everything stills.

The dust starts to settle, and I hear movement again. Surrounding me is now a small trench, created by the force of the storm that I just released from my body. Two of the four horsemen lay at my feet, their bodies burned and torn from the lightning. The light of the sun bursts through, and with it, I see the damage I have done. A large chunk of the army is dead, the other two horsemen get thrown back, and the Archivist lay on the ground, stirring.

'Mother, Gengi, are you okay?'

A flash of power and my mother is standing beside me, Gengi soon follows. They have grabbed blades from the dead.

'We fight until we cannot, and if we die today, then it will be as warriors, not prisoners.' Gengi pounds on his chest like a beast.

'You are always so dramatic, my large friend.' I smile at him, this incredible human who has matched me in combat and stuck with me through it all since then. 'Let us fight!'

I grab the *Senso* blade off the dead leader of the Four. I feel its power hum through me, much like the elements did during the storm I created. The remaining soldiers rise and start to charge. In just a few breaths, all hell breaks loose.

I blast a wave of wind through a group of advancing soldiers. Their bodies fly backwards like rag dolls. My mother, who is at my back, calls upon the rain and snow, collecting it into a huge ball of ice. She releases it and uses the wind to fire it toward another group who get crushed in an icy death. Gengi is back to being the master of arms I knew in the arena. He dispatches three soldiers with ease with his duel swords. It is almost like he moves a little too fast for a human.

'Mother. What happens if we combine powers? Will it explode?' I shout while thrusting *Senso* through the heart of another enemy.

'I have no idea, your father and I didn't dare risk it.'

'It's time for risks,' Gengi shouts as he holds off another three dark soldiers. 'If you are going to do something, I recommend you make haste. I am good, but two-hundred soldiers could be a bit much.'

I absorb the sun, flashing forward and back into the ranks of men and women intent on our demise. It causes confusion, and the once fierce-looking army seems to be flailing around like an angry child. Yet, I fear that in a few moments, they will overwhelm us. Can I call upon another storm? Or are Gengi and my mother too close for it this time? I ask the winds to wrap around me as four arrows make flight towards me. The winds catch the missiles, swirling them around my body and back from whence they came. Two of the archers are speared and fall, the arrows striking true. The other two manage to feint by mere inches, avoiding the missiles by a whisper. My mother flies around the battlefield with such grace and speed, making quick work of all those who dare fight her. She is like a woman possessed. Her thin blade slicing through all that get in her path. My mother is a master of combining her powers and weapon as one fluid movement. I should have trained more with her, and she makes it seem so natural. I watch as she spins in a deadly flurry of strikes, another five warriors dropping to the ground, lifeless.

Gengi, if he is a human, is fighting as I have never seen before. He twirls and spins death as bodies pile up around him. He blocks an opponent to his front while simultaneously rending the throat of another assailant without looking behind him. How does he know where his enemies are like that? The winds speak to us in their whispers, but he doesn't have our powers?

I wake from my trance of watching Gengi fighting by a bellow of two voices in harmony. 'We must kill all Nephilim, Onoskelis demands that you die.' They leap into combat, a little too high for humans. They strike out at me simultaneously, as if both of them know exactly what the other is about to do and move in complete harmony. *Senso* is as light as a feather, and with some help from the breeze, my arms move incredibly fast, blocking both blows. Yet they persist, their attacks keep pressing me back, and in the corner of my eye, I see the Archivist running.

'Mother! The Archivist, he is escaping.'

She turns to see him entering his building and flashes over to join me in battling the two horsemen.

'Jacob, capture the wind and let it flow around us four. I have a plan. Gengi, we need you.'

'I'm a little busy right now,' he shouts while fending off no less than five. He slices the head off one and retreats to us. 'Okay, now what?'

I start to swirl the wind around us, forming it into a furious tornado to create a barrier between them and us. I see one soldier try to stick his blade in the torrent of wind, and his weapon instantly gets torn from his hand and tumbles into the other waiting warriors. My mother crouches, and I understand what she is trying to do.

'Get behind me, Gengi,' I warn the big man. 'Make yourself as small as possible, make sure as much of you is covered as possible.'

'Covered! By you? That is like trying to hide a horse behind a sheep!'

'Just do it, and quickly,' I shout.

My mother absorbs the sun. More and more, she generates heat. The gazing eye of it focuses on her, burning the ground we stand on. Her whole body starts to glow.

'Jacob, when I tell you, bring the winds where we stand, and when ready, release it in a wave.'

'Okay! Just tell me when.'

Her body starts to glow brighter than the sun itself, too bright for my eyes. I am forced to close them, but the light seems to penetrate even when they are tightly shut.

'I think I'm going blind, Telaá. Please hurry!' The Viking screams.

'Jacob, NOW!'

'I suck the wind back into us. The shards of stone and metal that lay about cut our bodies. I hear my mother and Gengi shouting in agony as the whirlwind gathers pace absorbing my mother's generated heat, causing the moisture to transform into powerful hot gases. The steam fires out with such ferocity that the army is instantly torn to shreds, the warriors disintegrating before our very eyes.

'Are you alive big man?' I ask.

'I am alive! I feel like I have a good tan, but I am alive.'

My mother relaxes, smiling, impressed by what we have just done. 'That was intense but just goes to show that we can combine our power. Imagine if all seven Nephilim were to do this. Onoskelis would stand no chance.'

I start to see movement on the ground. A few of the soldiers have survived but don't seem keen to fight. Out of dirt and chaos, I see the two horsemen rise.

'These guys are hard to kill,' Gengi says. 'Let's finish this.'

We army of three, ready ourselves.

The two horsemen charge us. Their silver blades slicing through the air at great speed. Gengi lurches out at one from my left, leaving himself open for the second horseman to duck through the opening and stab him in the leg. Gengi still doesn't drop. The horseman pulls the blade free, and the Viking barely winces. I slam my foot into the face of the attacker, assisted by the wind for extra power, and he stumbles back. My mother takes advantage of it, rolls behind him and thrusts her blade into the top of his spine, disconnecting his body from his brain. He slumps over, dead. The final horseman swings at me foolishly. He still hasn't figured out that the game is over. As I shift my weight and attack, he smiles. A trick! He wants me to think he is an open target so that he could take advantage of my split-second adjustment. He drives a hidden dagger deep into my side and instantly turns to Gengi.

'Stop this now! Or else your mother dies,' says the Archivist who now emerges from the building where we had our first meeting. 'You fools, I don't run from battle when I have the means to finish it so easily.'

We all stop. For a few moments, the world seemed to go quiet. The horseman's blade pointed at Gengi, the dagger still protruding from his side and my mother facing her husbands killer.

'I am sick of this, goodbye Nephilim.' The Archivist fires his gun.

For the first time, I flash forward while absorbing the sun. My father used to tell me that the world continues to travel at the same speed even when flash move, yet at this moment, the world seems to slow down to almost a halt. I see the shot from the gun shifting towards my mother, faster than anything I have seen before. As I move, I swirl the wind around my wrist, reaching out and drawing in as much as I can. There is no explosion as I combine my powers this time. I don't know why, but the elements allow me to use them together. They become one within me. I race towards the shot, moving faster than lightning, catching the missile in my hand merely inches before it meets my mothers head. I fire the breeze out back toward the Archivist, firing the small piece of metal right back from where it came. He doesn't have time to move; it strikes him hard and leaves a hole where his temple used to be. The last horseman stalls, and at that moment, Gengi drives his sword into the stunned creature's throat. The world goes still once again.

A few moments after the chaos ends, the slaves start to emerge from the buildings they were hiding in. They seem unsure at first, but Gengi rushes to them, getting to work unchaining them.

'How did you do that, Jacob?' My mother asks.

'I don't know. It just felt like I could, like the elements called to me and told me to use them together.'

'That's not supposed to be possible, my son. The Nephilim have restrictions placed on their powers else they become too much for even the angels to control.'

'I am the son of two Nephilim, Mother. Perhaps this is why it is forbidden?'

'If only your father were here, he would know what it was, I am sure of it.'

'At least he can rest properly now that *Senso* is back with us.' I pass the blade over to my mother. 'You are the leader of the Nephilim now, Mother.' I bow to her, and she responds in kind.

'I hope I can do your father the credit he deserves.'

'Mother, the way you fought out there. You were unlike anything I had seen before. He is up there, not only smiling but impressed. You fight like a demon.'

Gengi releases all of the slaves and walks back to us. 'They need guidance. Most have been slaves since childhood. What shall we do with them all?'

'Gengi, the first thing we must do is destroy this place and all that is in it. Grab all the horses, make the people ready, and pull together all the rations you can. As soon as we can, we leave.'

He leaves instantly. He stands on a table to address the crowd.

'Today is your day of freedom, friends. You are released from the tyranny of the Archivist. Today brings a change in life. Today is the day that you choose your destiny, and today is the day you see the world. I beckon you all, do not let this experience make you sour. Let it make you strong. You have already endured more than most, and you have come out on top. Now is your chance to become something, become someone, now is your time to start living!' Gengi shouts at them. 'Now, my friends, grab what you can, get horses for the frail, get food for all, and as soon as you are ready, we leave for this new world.'

'Hail Frostmane, freer of the innocent!' The crowd's shout in response. 'Hail to the angels that watch over us!'

We spend hours preparing the two-hundred odd people for departure. They grab almost everything they can. Armour, weapons, food and supplies. They seem to follow Gengi around like lost pups, in awe of him.

'Frostmane?' I ask the Viking.

'Aye. It would seem they gave me a nickname because of my furs.'

'What about the Viking?'

'The Viking died here, Jacob. That life is over. If I am to help these people, and others like them, my arena life must be forgotten.'

'Frostmane is a kingly name, my friend. I like it.' The big man smiles from ear to ear. I think secretly he loves the attention. Plus, a name like Frostmane sounds great, and I'm sure the ladies will love it too. 'My mother and I will stay behind for a few moments after you leave. There is something we need to do.'

Gengi bows to me and heads off to gather his people.

With Gengi at the forefront, the small army leaves, leading his new band of people with him.

'Are you ready, Mother?'

'I am. Let's wipe this vile place from history.'

We both gather the wind around us, replicating the whirlwind we made during the battle. This time we aim at the mountain itself. Blasting its side and bringing boulders, snow and destruction toppling on to the fortress and completely submerging it. All the books and plans burnt, and with them, the ideas and devices that should have never returned. The guns are thrown back into the smelters, and the tanks disassembled. No one should have access to such weapons of destruction.

We bury the whole place and hope that in time, people will forget it ever existed.

'What now?' I ask my Mother.

Chapter 34 – Home

We make slow progress as we push ourselves back down the snowy mountains: Gengi, my mother and I leading the group back to my home. Most of them have donned the garments of the dead soldiers that once guarded them. It makes me feel strange. We have spent days being pursued by people dressed in those outfits; now we have a couple of hundred of them following our lead into a new world for them. They are hardy folk, though, none of them complaining about the cold and all taking it in turns to use the horses, and although it is freezing, I haven't heard a single peep. If anything, they are the happiest I can imagine they have been before, especially as most have never left the compound.

Gengi has taken to the role of being a leader very quickly. They all look up to him as their saviour. He keeps them smiling with stories of his gladiatorial days and talks about the city of Neodias. They all seem in awe of him. He was a showman in the arena, so why not be one now.

'Gengi!' I cut him off another story about a victory in the arena that saw him crowned champion for the tenth time.

'Jacob, my friend. You interrupt me in full flow. Are you sickening of my stories?' He chuckles, rolling his eyes to his adoring crowds.

'No, Mr Frostmane. I have a question. In the arena, you only used hammers, yet seeing you work duel blades, I can see that you have far more prowess with those than you ever did your favoured weapon?'

'I never told you the hammer was my favourite weapon. I was told to use it to make me more Viking, which made me more appealing to the crowds. Duel swords have always been my favourite.'

'I'm learning a great many things from you, Frostmane.' I will use his new name as often as I can. Something about it feels right.

He nods to me. 'No doubt there will be a lot more to learn, my friend.'

Gengi continues with his stories, adding the most recent events to it and how he met me and my prowess in the arena. The adoring crowd look at me with glee. I don't take to the attention as well as

Gengi, but it is quite nice to have people look up to me instead of trying to kill me for a change. For the first time since my father was murdered, I feel a sense of hope take root.

We make slow progress, but after weeks of walking, we finally see my homestead. The farms and fields swiftly draw me back to my childhood. The fond memories of my father and I training, the miles upon miles I ran from this town to the next, the smell of the breakfast my mother had prepared as I stirred from my slumber in the morning. I can't help but smile. I glance at my mother, and I feel that she is having similar thoughts to me. A fondness for the quiet and calm that once was. Can we ever go back to that, I wonder?

'It's good to be home, Mother.'

'It is. Although I feel like it's different now. A bit of it was lost when your father was killed, and despite avenging his death, I fear that it will never truly return.'

I grab my mothers hand, clutching it in my own. 'We have people to adopt now. Homes to build, and a community to bond.'

'This isn't something we should have, Jacob. We need to rally the others, the remaining six are out there, and we need to use *Senso* to finish Onoskelis before his corruption takes hold of all the minds of men.'

'The summoning? We must go?'

'Yes, my Son. You are now a part of this, and I fear that we will need you and your exceptional power to defeat him. We must leave as soon as possible.'

'I can't. We must wait for word from Bipin and Yerkasha.'

'The fate of men is our task. We cannot abandon them all for the sake of only two.'

'Then you should go ahead. I'm sorry, but I can't just leave without them. They both helped to save my life, and now I must make sure that they are okay. Bipin went against the rules of heaven to save her for me.'

'Okay, Son. Two months to help build homes for these people, then I will leave, with or without you.' She squeezes my hand. She knows what it's like to be in love. She broke all the rules to be with my father. What am I, though? I am more than a Nephilim. My powers have surpassed my parents, and the four horsemen couldn't feel my presence. What did my parents create when they rebelled against the rules to have me?

I step into my house, leaving Gengi to round up the people and get pitching tents to rest. The other townsfolk have come to greet us and have offered their hand to help these people build homes here. My house looks almost identical to what it was before it got burned to the ground. The shadows still feel a little darker than they were before. Knowing that I gained revenge for my father's death, wielding *Senso* and that we destroyed all of those weapons in that godforsaken place has helped it to grow a little lighter.

My mother sets to work instantly, and the familiar smells come flooding back. I enter my room to find it is much the same. Only the pictures are missing. Those images of the elements are imprinted in my memories forever. I don't need them on my walls anymore. The sun pierces through my window as it did before, and I open them to allow the breeze in. I allow it to swirl around me and my room, almost like it has come to check it out as my protector.

'Food is ready, Jacob.' My mother calls, and I rush out to see what she has prepared.

'Rice balls and eggs! Oh, how I missed you.' I say to my plate. My mother just smiles softly. Yet, an air of sadness still looms over her. She is right; we cannot stay here. It is no longer our home, and we have so much more to do. We must gather the Nephilim and call them to act before all of humankind falls into corruption. That is why the Nephilim were placed on this planet, is it not? Yet, something that the Archivist said to me still lingers in my brain.

Nearly two months pass without word from our friends and my love. I have searched the plains and neighbouring villages but have heard nothing of them. I can only assume the worst, but a small part of me feels that Bipin has kept her safe.

We have built so many homes, and the once quiet little farmstead is buzzing with people. They have all got to work on various things. The farmland has spread, animals of all sorts have been tamed and brought in. Many of the people have been learning from the other townsfolk. Some have been sewing, some baking, and some have been training with Gengi and me. They have adapted to their new lives very quickly, and the warriors we have been training have proven to be strong and quick. All those years of smashing and bending metal have given them all the groundwork for becoming exceptional fighters.

Many have started calling Gengi King Frostmane. We, of course, have joined them. We know that we are to leave and perhaps never come back, so this now considerably larger town will need a leader. So, King Frostmane, he has become. My mother and I prepare to leave, heading south to the desert for the summoning. We pack food, weapons and armour, but light enough for us to move quickly or hide should another army of dark soldiers come searching for us.

I have been honing my powers during the two months that have passed — working on combining the elements as one. I no longer need to hide them from regular folk as most of the people surrounding us have seen them. Gengi and I have trained to help him fight those with powers, just in case more like the four horsemen arrive on our doorstep. His skills grow substantially, as do my own, working the elements in ways I never knew I could, and yet I feel there is still more power to be had. It's like the elements call to me continually now, urging me for more and more, begging me to use them and push myself. I combine wind with rain and find that to some level. I can almost create walls of water. I can also now change the heat of the water by combining it with the sun. I can't make it boil, but nice warm water I can produce at will. I want to journey back into the snowy mountains to see if I could use this combination to melt the ice as it falls. I still have no control over them after they have struck the earth, but that's okay.

Too much power could be dangerous, especially when it's untamed.

'Are you ready to go, Jacob?' My mother asks.

'As ready as I ever will be. It seems like only yesterday I left to find Father's killer. Now I am off to find six people who I have never known, in the hope we can stop Onoskelis.'

'I am sorry that this has happened to you, my Son. Perhaps this is why we were not meant to have you. Perhaps this is the will of the gods for us breaking the rules.'

Suddenly, a shadow looms in front of the doorway: a familiar one with a huge silhouette almost as big as the door frame itself.

'Bipin!' I shout, racing towards the door as the watcher steps inside.

He bows to us, looking no worse for wear. 'Jacob, Telaá. It is good to see you both again.'

My mother smiles at the giant watcher and offers him a seat.

'I bring both good and bad tidings, my friends.'

I interrupt him, my needing to know getting the better of me. 'Yerkahsa… does she live?'

'She does.'

At that moment, I see two more figures walk through the door. They are both shrouded with capes made of patched greens and browns, and I feel that if they didn't want to be seen, they wouldn't be. They take off their camouflage, revealing their identities to us all.

'Hello, Jacob,' says a voice I know too well.

I jump from my seat and rush into Yerkasha's arms, her embrace warming me instantly. I pull away and gaze into her jade eyes, and they are beautiful.

'My love! Are you well? Are you hurt? Are you hungry?'

'Do not fret, Jacob. Bipin and this man you might know have kept me well protected.'

I glance over to the other figure, seeing a familiar face. 'Ajax?'

'Samurai.' He bows. 'Excuse the beard, Bipin suggested that it would help me not to be recognised should we run into some undesirables.'

'Thank you. Thank you for helping them to escape.'

'We helped each other, my old friend. Bipin is quite a crack shot with that bow of his. I simply know the secret passages around the city.'

I collect some more chairs and ask the three of them to sit and relax. My mother prepares food and Bipin some of his incredible tea. They tell me about the journey they went through. Bipin saving both the others on multiple occasions. Ajax was hiding them in his home for the first week. They waited for the chaos to subside. Bipin warning them that darkness was looming over the city, and only now did he realise that the darkness must have been Onoskelis. We relay our battle in return, telling him of the army of dark soldiers and the Archivist. The horrible weapons he was creating and the armoured vehicles he called tanks.

Finally, we tell him about my powers. Combining them should not be possible, and he feels that this was not something that the gods had planned. Perhaps this is something new. The watcher looks at the packs on the floor, overflowing with food and weapons.

'I take it you are leaving,' asks the Watcher.

'We leave for the summoning, Bipin. If Onoskelis is back, we must get the other Nephilim together.'

'You have the blade, I see. This is good. You must have been successful in your task.'

'You surely know that already?' I ask.

'I... I am just a normal man now, Jacob. The agents of the almighty contacted me. They told me I must return to heaven as I had got myself involved in human actions. I refused, so they stripped me of my power of vision.'

'Can you still use that bow of yours?' Telaá asks, lifting the weapon that is almost twice her size.

'I can.'

'Then you can still help us. You will know the last-known locations of the others. We leave to find them today.'

'There is a problem, Telaá. Before I lost my powers, I lost the sense of three of the Nephilim. I have no idea if they still live.'

'Then we must go as soon as possible!'

I stand to agree with my mother. 'So. Whos coming?'

The room stands in unison.

'Then, we leave now. We head south into the desert, and we find what is left of the summoning, banding together with those who we can muster, then we kill Onoskelis.'

End of Book One

Thank you

There are so many people to thank for making my first novel come to light. So, if you wouldn't mind baring with me for a moment, I shall attempt to thank them all.

First and foremost, I would like to thank my friend Katy for believing in me and telling me I am good enough for my Master's degree. That was such a huge turning point.

My Master's tutor, Amy (who wrote the Biggerers), was a constant source of teachings and inspiration.

My proofreaders. My mother, Denise, my father, John, Katrin, who helped me start this adventure so late in life. And my friend Jaimie, who has been a constant source of support and love.

There are others who helped me along the way, but too many to mention. I hope you all know how much you helped me, and I hope that this is the first of many (at least two more) books in the future.

Printed in Great Britain
by Amazon

10382810R00220